Centra
W9-DDY-296
11828
FIC WEN
Across the pond

# Across The Pond

S.E. Wendel

# Across the Pond
Freshmen: Book #1

Written by S.E. Wendel



Published by EPIC Press™
PO Box 398166
Minneapolis, MN 55439



Printed in the United States of America.



Cover design by Kali VanZuilen
Images for cover art obtained from iStockPhoto.com
Edited by Kirsten Rue

Library of Congress Cataloging-in-Publication Data

Names: Wendel, S.E., author.
Title: Across the pond / by S.E. Wendel.
Description: Minneapolis, MN : EPIC Press, [2017] | Series: Freshmen
Summary: It's overwhelming, to say the least, when the two biggest dreams Carson Fields has ever had come true all in the same day: not only does he leave his rural Lake Tahoe home to start school at Oxford University, but then he meets the childhood sweetheart he thought had gotten away. But living so far from home isn't all Carson dreamed it would be. And neither, it turns out, is his dream girl.
Identifiers: LCCN 2016931762 | ISBN 9781680763447 (lib. bdg.) | ISBN 9781680763300 (ebook)
Subjects: LCSH: College students—Fiction. | Identity—Fiction. | Interpersonal relations—Fiction. | Young adult fiction.
Classification: DDC [Fic]—dc23
LC record available at http://lccn.loc.gov/2016931762

EPICPRESS.COM

*To Amy and Larry, without whom*
*Oxford would have only been half as memorable*

Carson Fields shrugs away from his mother's incessant, fussing fingers as they try to straighten the collar of his jacket. He resists the urge to tap his foot as he waits with his parents near the baggage carousel. If he'd had his way, they would already be walking to the awaiting bus, one bag in hand. But no. His mother had packed him two suitcases, stuffed to the brim. What use she thought he'd have for his father's old Packers jersey he couldn't say.

"Well they play *football* there," she'd said.

Carson hadn't the heart to correct her, but it was one of the many reasons he'd chosen to attend college approximately five thousand miles away.

With a little "Aha!" Carson's father pounces on the second suitcase, lifting it off the carousel with a mighty heave. Clicking up the handle, he gives Carson a wink before wheeling it away from the other passengers on their international flight.

Carson checks his wristwatch then wishes he hadn't. Running an agitated hand through his hair, which feels brittle thanks to recycled airplane air, he says, "We gotta hurry up; the bus leaves in ten minutes!"

"Right," his father says, scanning the directions overhead. "This way, I think."

Following dutifully behind, Carson just hopes there aren't any knickknack booths between them and the bus. His mother never could resist a knickknack booth, as the cluttered cabinet in their computer room back home—boasting shelves full of snow globes, bobble heads, and all manner of commemorative mugs—can attest to.

They navigate the escalators and hallways at a hurried power walk, Carson feeling downright bewildered by the labyrinthine Heathrow. Finally, they spill out into a roofed parking lot with bus-length spaces. Only one sits in the first row, and Carson breathes a sigh of relief to see Ms. Billings, one of the coordinators for the American Scholars Abroad program, talking to the driver.

Catching sight of them, Ms. Billings turns and smiles as Carson's father lets out a loud, friendly, "Hello, there!"

"Oh, lovely!" Ms. Billings says as the Fields come scurrying along. "Now everyone's here, and we can get started!"

She hustles Carson and his mother onto the bus as his father helps the driver load suitcases. Hopping up the steps, Carson realizes with no small amount of chagrin that they're the last to arrive. The bus is already filled with excited, anxious faces, and Carson slumps into the last empty seat, close to the front, slouching so that the people behind can't see his burning ears.

Nearly missing the bus—not the way he wanted to start his first year at the University of Oxford.

His mother slides in next to him, and he shifts in his seat closer to the window, jamming his hands deep into his jacket pockets, just in case she has any ideas of holding hands for the hour drive up to Oxford.

His father, Ms. Billings, and the driver are the last to board. Once his father is situated in the seat in front of him, Ms. Billings takes the little handheld radio from the driver. Into it she says, "Hello everyone! I'm so excited for us to get started. It's going to be little over an hour to reach Oxford. In the meantime," she sways as the bus driver puts it in reverse, "I'll be passing around some material for you. Nothing to sign, thankfully, though Joe's driving is smooth as silk. I've got a map here with all the colleges highlighted. Not all of you are at the same college, though we did try to cluster you. When we arrive, I'll be directing you to your college and then I'll come check in on you later, to make sure I didn't lose anyone down the Thames!" She gets a few nervous laughs for that. "I've also got some pamphlets about your college, along with papers with your registration numbers, IDs, all that good stuff."

Giving the radio back to the driver, Ms. Billings starts to expertly work her way down the aisle with a large stack of papers.

"Yes, Fields," she says when Carson, the first up, gives her his name. She shifts the papers in her arms, leafing through. "Put these in alphabetical order. I guess it'd be too much to expect everyone to *sit* in alphabetical order," she says with a laugh. Hitting about the middle of the stack, she extracts a small packet. "Here you are."

Ms. Billings puts the packet into his expectant, slightly clammy hands, and Carson immediately flips to the map. There's a little red X on a section of High Street, then a dotted red line down several more roads, finally ending with a circled Jesus College.

His enthusiasm ebbs when his mother tips the map toward her with a finger. "I don't understand why you're getting split up into different colleges. I thought you were all going to Oxford."

"We are," Carson says. "Oxford is spread out over a bunch of separate colleges."

"Is Jesus the writing college?"

He shrugs. "No. It's not really based on subject matter."

"Then how is it organized?"

"It isn't, really."

She frowns. "That's not how we do it."

He shrugs again, having already figured out where this is headed. "Well they've been doing colleges a lot longer than we have."

"Hmph," she says. It's the noise she makes when she hasn't come up with a counterargument *yet*, so he shouldn't think he's gotten away. Her put-a-pin-in-it noise.

Carson glues his eyes to the clogged streets of London. He knows from his careful research and slight addiction to Google Maps that Heathrow is outside of London proper, that they won't cross over London Bridge or spy Big Ben on the drive out into the English countryside. Still, it's slightly disappointing to settle for the meandering concrete of airport terminals and gangways. It *is* fun, albeit disorienting, to be driving on the wrong side of the road, however.

He smiles to himself as they enter a roundabout, going almost all the way through before spilling out onto another road. They pass cars and buses and throngs of people before finally, after coming out from yet another concrete tunnel, Carson spots green fields. England opens up before them, and he doesn't care that he's craning his neck like an idiot, trying to take in the soft, rolling hills. He breathes easier, the thrumming panic of having almost missed the bus subsiding.

Before long they spy country pastures, streams, and even a few hamlets. He can hear the excited murmuring of the rest of the American students behind him, can feel as they do that they stand on the threshold of an adventure.

Carson refuses to let his mother's scowl dampen his mood. He knows she gets carsick easily, and driving on the opposite side of the road is probably partly to blame for her dark look, but he also knows she's brooding. The hour is drawing closer. Soon she and his father will be on a return flight to San Francisco, leaving Carson, the eldest of their four children, behind in a foreign country, with foreign customs, to study foreign subjects with foreigners. Carson can't wait.

He smiles to himself, though, to see that his father is fast asleep. His father can sleep anywhere. He slept through most of the ten-hour flight over, something Carson is keenly jealous of, especially when the green hills begin to blur together and he feels the pull of sleep. His brain still thinks it's close to midnight—which it is, at home in California—whereas here it's a bright new day. Carson doesn't know if he's ever felt this tired at eight in the morning before.

After a few more rolling pastures, the bus mounts a pass between two large hills, and the road descends into Oxfordshire. He can see it spread out below; the ancient college town is waiting for him.

The drive to the airport, the flight, the bus ride here seems short compared to the half hour it takes to get to downtown Oxford. He can feel it when they turn onto High Street. He marvels, eyes wide, as the gray stone gates of colleges pass by with their huge wooden doors. People mill about in the streets, ducking into colleges, shops, and cafes. Most of the buildings stand at least four stories high, and Carson can't quite believe the bus driver manages to navigate this narrow maze with such a hulking vehicle.

His pulse thrums in his neck as they turn into a bus depot, where other brightly colored buses are dropping off and collecting passengers. As the bus driver eases them into their parking space,

Ms. Billings hops up off her seat next to Carson's father and says with a clap, "We're here!"

He's positively floating, and nothing can bring him down. Not his mother's more-than-obvious dubiousness as she looks about the bus depot, as if that's where he'll be going to school; not his father going on with the bus driver, helping unload not only Carson's baggage but everyone else's, making sure that the Fields are, again, last; not the fact that this new place is an explosion of sights, sounds, and noise, all crowding in front of his senses, competing for attention. Cobblestones and pigeons and windowed business fronts all scream difference from his quiet alpine home in Tahoe.

Carson wheels one of his unruly suitcases out of the bus depot. He can hear Ms. Billings giving tour-like directions, but he can't quite catch what she says other than the bus depot is called Gloucester Green.

His mother frowns. "That sounds like the name of a golf course."

His father chuckles.

Carson attempts not to roll his eyes.

His heart leaps into his throat again when he sees groups are beginning to break off after showing their maps to Ms. Billings.

"I'll walk with you," she says to the Fields. "People always seem to think Jesus is hard to find." She and Carson share a wry smile over that.

They walk up a slight incline before coming upon a busy intersection. After a few more minutes of walking, an old church tower peeks out from the rows of prim, more modern buildings. Ms. Billings calls it St. Michael at the North Gate. "Not far now."

They turn onto a wide pedestrian promenade boasting an eclectic array of cafes, pubs, a Starbucks, boutiques, restaurants, and tourist traps. Ms. Billings walks ahead to answer the question of another student, and Carson catches that yes, the store called Boots is a pharmacy, basically the equivalent of a CVS back home.

They walk along the length of a college, the old stones rising some five stories to ornate steeples. He spies ancient-looking weather vanes and old leaded windows that open up onto the side street below. From the noise filtering down to him, he guesses they are dorm rooms.

Turning right at the end of the alley, Carson sees that they've just found Turl Street, and the familiar name orients his mental Google map. To his right is the huge wooden door of Jesus College, thrown open to allow suitcases easy access into an entryway.

The Fields cram into the small stone entryway as Ms. Billings pops into a lobby. A little gate prevents further access into the college, but does allow a sweeping view of a pristine quadrangle. The neat building facades form an almost square around a perfectly mown lawn with stone walkways crisscrossing it.

Ms. Billings comes to stand in the doorway with a little box of card keys and a clipboard. "Alright, one at a time, I'll give you your room keys. I've got a map here with some rules and procedures that the college wants you to have. There will be a more formal orientation this evening, so don't worry about anything other than getting settled." She turns her smile onto Carson, who's closest to the lobby. "Three-oh-two," she says, handing him the keys.

He takes the card key, and, in a bit of a daze, passes through the lobby with his parents, finally out into the quadrangle. They head down the main path, which leads them to a set of sharp steps. The suitcases bang against the stairs as they haul them up and then across an impossibly old wooden floor. His head on a swivel, he spies the dining hall to his right. He doesn't catch much in passing, but sees a long room with equally long tables, matching china, and old, dark wooden walls sporting portraits, one of which looks to be Queen Elizabeth I herself.

Down another set of steps and they're in

a second quadrangle. They follow the map Ms. Billings gave them and skirt around the lawn, passing through an archway on the west side into a long courtyard. This part of the college looks newer, more concrete than stone, and some of the doors here are fiberglass rather than wood.

Carson's father holds up the map again. He points to another set of stairs and says, "Up we go."

The odyssey of stairs has only just begun when they realize what three-oh-two means: third floor, room two. He silently curses every unnecessary thing his mother packed yet again as he hauls the second suitcase after his father.

His shoulders are all in knots, his arms screaming, a slight line of perspiration gathering at his hairline when they finally walk through another door into a carpeted hallway lined with numbered doors that are all thrown open. Excited chatter fills the air, and Carson lets it swirl around him. He forgets his aches and sweaty hairline, leading the short way to room 302.

He enters a small anteroom. A narrow door leads into an equally narrow bathroom while a chest of drawers takes up the whole wall next to him. A movement through a second open door catches his eye.

A tall boy with shaggy blonde hair looks over at him and smiles. He's wearing a T-shirt under a blazer and rolled jeans. With an easy gait, he walks from the room into the entryway to offer his hand.

"You're the American, then?" He has a British accent.

Carson blinks, remembers to smile, and then shakes the boy's hand. He smells like fine aftershave and the outdoors. "That's me. Carson."

"Anderson," he says. "But they call me Anders."

By "they" he means his parents, who wave from his room.

"How're things in the States?" Anders's mother asks from the threshold.

"Falling apart without us, no doubt," says Carson's father with an easy smile.

Anders and his parents chuckle at that. "Come by when you're done in there," Anders says with a nod toward Carson's door.

"Sure thing."

Swiping the key through the card reader, a little green light flashes with a *click*, and he opens the door to his new life.

The room is cozy. A neatly made bed takes up a corner of the room, with a large desk and chair set against the far wall dominating most of the space. In a little niche next to the door are a wardrobe and dresser. Light splashes onto the forest-green carpet through a huge set of bay windows. Sitting below the windows are two plush chairs separated by a little table loaded with a tea tray bearing all the necessaries.

He breathes in the smell of fresh laundry as his parents edge around him to get in. His father does a low whistle, but his mother is uncharacteristically quiet. She says nothing as they begin unpacking, and Carson doesn't press her. She won't ruin this for him.

As he passes from his room toward the bathroom to safely stow his toothbrush, a flash of golden hair catches his eye from across the hall. He turns his head just as the girl whose hair it was turns to look at him. Their eyes meet.

His heart thuds painfully in his chest. "Anneliese."

Head swimming with memories of the childhood summers they spent together in Tahoe before she walked out of his life four years ago without a proper goodbye, Carson's throat clogs with a jumble of exclamations at seeing her here now. She seems equally stunned to see him, so it's Carson's father who breaks the silence. Coming up behind him to see what the fuss is about, Carson's father lets out a happy chuckle, crosses the threshold, and wraps Anneliese up in a bear hug.

"Anneliese! What're the odds? Are you going to school here too?"

Anneliese manages to stammer out a response, but Carson still can't make his feet move. Today was supposed to be about beginnings, starting fresh. He isn't sure what to do now, with the past staring at him from across the hallway.

Carson shoves his hands into his pockets and forces a smile onto his face as his mother straightens his jacket collar for the third time that morning. He refuses to look her in the eyes and see the tears there, because he knows if his mother cries, he'll, at the very least, get misty.

The long weekend has come to an abrupt end, and now that he's all moved into his dorm and has trekked through Oxford with his parents and the other ASA students, it's time. Time to start his life—or, at least, the rest of his life. He waits for it impatiently, but right that hot second, he struggles with a jumble of apprehension, guilt, wistfulness, and a whole array of other negative emotions he's shocked to feel. He pushes these feelings down until he's left with only a mildly choked feeling deep in his throat.

It doesn't help that only a few feet away stands Anneliese, saying goodbye to her own mother. He glances at her over his mother's head and sees she's stiffly receiving one last goodbye hug.

His father claps him on the back and gives his shoulders a squeeze in a sideways hug.

"Now, don't be a stranger," his father says, rumpling his hair. "We didn't buy you that international phone for nothing."

Carson nods, putting on another smile to force away the sudden aching in his heart. "No worries there."

"And remember to let us know if you need more allowance. The exchange rate's murder right now, but it'll probably come back down soon."

Assuring his father he'll be the model of frugality, they nod and leave the money talk there. Neither likes to talk money, but moving overseas required several uncomfortable discussions about finances. Carson had done his best to get scholarships and grants. While he'd been able to cover most of it himself, the difference and money to survive on had come from a combination of his savings account, bolstered by two summer jobs, and his parents.

His mother takes his face in her hands, and he receives her soft kiss against his cheek. "Be a good boy," she tells him. "Make lots of friends and don't be late to class. But remember, you can always come home, whenever you want. Okay?"

He nods. "Yeah, Mom. I know." He wraps her up in a hug, resting his chin on the top of her head. "I'll miss you."

His father gathers the two of them together in his arms, and within that warm embrace, Carson suddenly feels far away from his parents. He's stunned a little, having thought he'd be happy to feel that way.

When his parents take a step back, he misses the contact. They look over to where Anneliese and her mother stand, and his father waves. "It's great to see you again."

Anneliese's mother nods, forcing a smile.

He watches as his parents mount the bus steps, an apprehensive hollow spot in his chest. When the bus begins backing up, he spots his mother's face in one of the middle windows. She waves to him.

"Hey."

He turns to find Anneliese standing beside him, and a new rush of emotions surges through him. If someone had told him he'd experience such a kaleidoscope of emotions today, he would've argued no human was capable of feeling so much all at once.

"Hey," he says as the bus departs from Gloucester Green.

She holds herself stiff, her narrow shoulders square and rigid. She's barely grown in the four years since he last saw her. Her honey-colored hair, long now, is pulled back into a loose braid. He looks at her face, though her sky-blue eyes won't rise to meet his, and sees she still has those freckles adorning her cheeks and the ridge of her nose. He finds, even four years later, that those freckles still strike him as cute as hell. Her hands disappear into the long arms of the oversized sweater she wears as she seems to wait.

Growing up, summertime had meant Anneliese. She came up with her parents to their summer cabin, two down from Carson's house, every summer until they were fourteen.

"Kind of unreal, isn't it?" he says with a small grin in her direction.

Her eyes flick up to him and he's rewarded with a smile. "Definitely hard to believe," she agrees.

"Lots of tears for you?"

"Not from my mother, but," she shrugs, "I didn't think she would."

"I didn't think my mom would ever stop. I still can't believe she let me do this."

"You're not going to be a little boy forever."

He finds his hands migrating back into his pockets, and they burrow like prairie dogs there, as far down as they can get. As their conversation dies with a lackluster fizzle, a million questions jump to mind, competing in his throat so that nothing ends up getting out: Why didn't she reach out to him after the cabin was sold? Where has she been? Why did she walk out of his life four years ago without a trace, only to reappear now?

He clears his throat. "Do you wanna get coffee?"

She nods, though she still isn't looking at him. "I could go for coffee. Though," she grins, "I haven't found anything I like here yet."

"It's pretty awful, isn't it? And they say *we* have bad coffee."

"Well, hopefully I find something soon—I'm quite the addict, really."

"Oh, yeah? Well you can't be worse than my old history teacher. Had a pot a day. Black."

She wrinkles her nose. "Okay, no, I'm not that bad." She flashes him a white-toothed smile. "And I have the teeth to prove it."

Their conversation carries them back to the

pedestrian-only promenade called Cornmarket Street.

"So where'll it be?" he asks.

Pulling out her phone, Anneliese begins typing away. The blue LED light reflects in her equally blue eyes, and in the small silence while she checks everywhere with a coffee shop, Carson again fights the urge to fling a volley of questions at her. He needs to be calm, cool, collected. He needs to get this right. He'd tried many times to find her on social media, but she never seemed to be there, so her physically standing beside him again is almost too good to be true. He lost Anneliese once—it couldn't be coincidence they'd come to the same country, same university, same college, same damn dorm building. It has to mean something. He loved her, inasmuch as a fourteen-year-old could love someone, and he wants to believe, despite his father's monologue about coincidence after seeing Anneliese in the hallway, that this is meant to be.

"There're a few places," she's saying, but it takes

a moment for his attention to click back into place. "This one looks interesting." She tilts the phone screen to show him the map.

"Sounds good," he says. "Besides, it's probably too early to admit defeat and just get Starbucks."

The street is rather crowded with end-of-the-season tourists, so they walk in companionable silence. Passing by the ancient tower of St. Michael at the North Gate, they're soon in the shadow of a multilevel building with an eclectic pattern of classical columns flanking broad windows with posters, signs, and books. A thrill of excitement jolts through him as he discovers a bookstore through the propped open glass doors. When they walk in, he sees the name, WATERSTONES, embossed across the door.

There are stacks of books, shelves of books, book arrangements, book posters, and piles and piles of books. A happy sort of euphoria settles over him as he looks with glazed eyes at the colorful paperbacks and glossy hardcovers. He's reaching for the newest bestseller, some new, "smashing" biography about Napoleon that he never knew he needed, when the golden glint of Anneliese's hair catches his eyes.

She's deftly weaving between the tables of books and other shoppers, headed for a small black staircase at the far side of the store. Vowing to return for Napoleon, Carson hurries to catch up. Hanging a left on the landing, they find a quaint café tucked neatly in a niche of the bookstore, the newest novels adorning the shelves around them.

The bright yellow walls of the café invite him to order more than he's hungry for, but the silent, nervous wait with Anneliese in line convinces him that anxiety-eating a muffin probably isn't the best thing to do. He clenches then unclenches his fists until Anneliese finishes making her order and it's his turn.

A few minutes later, they claim a table set against one of the large rectangular windows looking down onto the quiet, green churchyard of St. Mary Magdalene. Carson sets down his steaming paper coffee cup with an unceremonious clang of coins.

Anneliese grins at all the change and says, "They certainly do like their coins here."

Carson nods as he shoves them into his front pants pockets. "I think I'm going to have to get a separate wallet for them all, and it's only been three days!"

She giggles, and Carson is swept back to the summers of his childhood, romping around the crystalline Lake Tahoe. With her. "Look! Look at this!" Anneliese had said, waving him over to a moss-covered log where a few small fish swam in a shallow pool beneath. Her shadow crossed over them, spooking them. "Look at how shiny they are!" she said amid a flurry of giggles.

The memory makes him nervous again, and he runs his hands along the length of his thighs.

"So how've you been?" he asks finally, applauding himself for the diplomatic vagueness.

A small, terse grin adorns her mouth for a moment, but then her eyes, and the grin, fall.

"Alright. Moved around a lot. I'm happy to stay put for a few years," she says, rather forcefully.

Carson nods, though he can't relate in the slightest. Picking up and moving across not only the country, but the Atlantic Ocean was the most exciting thing anyone had done in his family for four generations, all the way back to old Jeb Fields, the cattle-rustler, notorious (if unlucky) gambler, womanizer, and all-around vagabond. Carson loves that his distant relative's gravestone, sitting in the graveyard of one of the numerous ghost towns littering the California-Nevada border, said only, *Jeb Fields, b. 1832 d. 1864, Died With His Boots On.*

The question of "What made you decide to come all the way over to Jolly Old England for school?" seems the safest. He's itching to know everything about her life during the past four years: Where has she lived? Where has she gone to school? What were her friends there like? Were they anything like him? Did she miss him? Did she remember their last day together, when they had sat under the vast

California sky and kissed each other in that inept fourteen-year-old way? Had she felt what that kiss did to him?

He's watching her mouth move, answering his question, but barely hears it. He's thinking of that evening, when the sky had been shot through with streaks of gold and lilac and midnight blue, when he'd pleaded in his head to whatever higher powers would listen for Anneliese to stay. With him.

"I guess, to sum up," she says, her lips tugged up at the edges by a grin as they always did when she realizes she's been monologuing, "I needed a change of scenery. I'm so used to it by now, with Mom moving us all over."

Carson lets an easy smile play across his face even though he doesn't have the feelings to match. "Well, you picked some fine scenery."

"Yes, I did," she says, looking at the broad window. "And what about you?"

"What?"

"What made you choose Oxford?"

"Oh. Same thing, I guess. Change of scenery." That was an understatement. If there were two more different places on the planet, they were the crisp alpine villages nestled against the snow-melted Lake Tahoe, and the cobblestoned mausoleums of learning that had existed long before his own country. "Home's a small place and I wanted to get out into the world."

The conversation falters again, and Carson wishes she would say something, ask something. He isn't used to the reserved person sitting across the table from him. He senses that it's more than being reserved—Anneliese sometimes retreats into the confines of her mind, a realm even Carson found difficult to enter. She's actually struggling to find words.

So Carson does what comes naturally to the eldest of four children: he redirects attention.

"So are you still doing photography? Oxford's a great subject to photograph."

She politely waits until he's finished to shake her

head. "No, not really. All my cameras are so old and fragile that they definitely wouldn't have survived the trip anyways."

He can't believe the words coming out of her mouth, but he tries to keep his face impassive. Anneliese always used to have a camera hanging around her neck. It started with one of those clunky, plastic, pink cameras with a Barbie logo. But when it was apparent she had a real passion, her parents allowed her to graduate to Canon and Nikon. Carson remembers Anneliese's bedroom at her parents' cabin; her gleaming photographs lined the walls, floor to ceiling, alongside pictures and posters she had clipped from magazines like *National Geographic*.

"How about you? Are you still writing your stories?"

He grins in spite of himself. She always called them "your stories."

"Yeah, I'm trying to keep up with it." He is, in fact, here to do only that—write. He's already had a little success back home, with two short stories featured in northern California literary journals. Now he's finally somewhere he can major in what he loves, be forced to produce what he loves, work constantly at what he loves. Damn it all if he can't come up with a masterpiece where Carroll, Tolkien, Lewis, and Pullman did theirs.

"Though," he says, "I'll admit, dragons feature a little less prominently these days."

She laughs. "That's a shame. You always had the best dragons."

"I've been beaten to the punch, unfortunately."

"You'll find your thing. I know it."

He warms at the praise. "Hopefully. Or die trying."

She arches an eyebrow. "Well, all the best authors die young. Half of them are more famous for dying than writing."

"True," he laughs. "I suppose that's what I'm really here for—a dark and sordid start to my tragic plight as a struggling writer."

Anneliese smirks at all the vocab words and looks about the bright bookstore, then back at him with a crooked smile. "Not exactly a seedy start to your bohemian lifestyle."

"No," he admits. Finding the girl that got away, however, might be.

Carson tries not to fidget as the class settles down, attention turning to Professor Vicks, who stands imperiously at the front of the class. He's flipping through the syllabus he gave them last class, returning to exactly where he left off.

"Let's get started," Professor Vicks projects. "I know Homer's been around for ages, but there isn't a minute to lose—I've millennia to teach but only three months to do it!"

Leaning against the head table behind him, Vicks once again goes over his expectations for the class, a summary of the reading schedule, and then gives them the grade breakdown. He answers questions about exams, a word that causes Carson's stomach to kick a little, before launching into a half-lecture on Homer's legacy.

Carson leans forward a little on his elbows, listening intently. He hopes his eyes aren't too wide with academic excitement.

"Yes, I see what time it is," Vicks says when the last minute of class ticks by. He tilts the watch face toward him and waits until the seconds finally run out and it's the top of the hour. Finally, a grin breaks out over his face, making Carson wonder how old he is. Vicks has one of those faces, a Clooney face, that seems to get better with age, yet makes it hard to put a precise number on.

"Alright then," Vicks says, pushing his glasses up onto his head, "have a good weekend. May you all have your own Odyssey." He seems pleased by the collective groan of the class over such a bad Classics joke.

Carson meets the eyes of the boy who sat next to him in class. They share a smile and he says,

"Hopefully that means we can take ten years to turn in the term paper."

Carson laughs and agrees.

"Nathan," he says, holding out a hand.

Carson takes it and shakes it, concentrating on being firm and maintaining eye contact, just as his father always told him to. "You can tell a lot about a person by their handshake," was one of his father's favorite dad-isms. Carson doesn't quite know what he can tell about Nathan, other than that his hands are slightly smaller than Carson's own, and clammier.

"Carson."

"You're one of the Americans."

"Yup."

"How're you liking it here?"

Now that's indeed the question. How *is* he liking it at Oxford? When he answers that question, he likes to tell himself he's getting on great, that things take a while to get used to, that it's normal to have difficulty making friends outside one's own roommate. When he answers that question truthfully, usually only in the small hours of the night when he's staring at the ceiling still waiting to get on English time, he admits that college—college in *England*—might be a tad overwhelming. Back home he wouldn't have to worry about which side of the street he needs to check before crossing, or where his passport is at all times. More than once he's stared blankly at English euphemisms whose meaning he hasn't the faintest idea about, since they weren't the ones used in the BBC dramas his sister Amy made him watch for what she called "preparation." Back home he would have the normal amount of college stress, just worrying about feeding himself and getting to class on time and doing the homework—

A jolt runs through him. Oh, lord, the homework—did he remember to do it? He can't quite believe he has any at all the first week, but he knows what's awaiting him when he steps back into his room. He's already thought about tacking the syllabus of each of his four classes up onto the wall so he can keep everything straight.

But he shouldn't be thinking about homework now. He needs to stay focused, in the present, with Nathan. He needs to make a friend so that he can stop hiding out in his room all night. After living in a house with five other people his whole life, a silent, empty room makes him uneasy.

So Carson grins as they start down the old stone steps to the second quadrangle. "It's great. Though, it rains a lot more than California."

"Ah."

Carson subdues his wince, watching the conversation take an unceremonious swan dive.

"What do you think of the class?" he forces himself to ask with a bland smile. Why couldn't he be as good with people as his brother, Jake? There was something to be said about being jealous of a ten-year-old's charisma.

"I think it's going to be brilliant," Nathan says,

warming to the topic. "But I should—it's my major."

"Oh, yeah? What's your area of interest?"

"Latin poetry, mostly. Always been a fan of the *Metamorphoses* and all."

Carson nods along as if he knows what that, or anything else on the syllabus other than Homer, is. He feels that to hold his head up in the literary world, he should have a working knowledge of all that's come before, which is why he's decided to take Classics. But between this, the Introduction to English, the World History, and the Intro to Philosophy class and all their respective required readings, he thinks his eyes might pop right out of his skull crying, "Freedom!" *Braveheart*-style.

"Are you taking Latin as a language too?" Carson asks.

"Yes." Nathan flashes him a smile. "Haven't done myself any favors, have I?"

Carson shakes his head as they walk through the arched portal into the narrow third quadrangle. It isn't really a true quadrangle, more like a narrow courtyard, connecting most of the living quarters of the students, a computer facility, and some of the newer classrooms.

"What about you?" Nathan asks, stopping before a doorway leading to one of the other dormitories.

"Oh, I'm an English major," he answers.

"Well you've come to the right place."

"So I hear."

After a grin, Nathan checks his watch. "I gotta run. I'll see you later?"

Carson nods. "Too early to start ditching class."

With a wave Nathan disappears into his dormitory, and Carson hops up the nearby stone steps, headed for his own. Feeling quite pleased with himself, Carson almost doesn't mind the stack of books that are, indeed, waiting for him when he opens his door.

Depositing his book and papers onto the wide desk, he looks about the freshly cleaned room. Perhaps one of the oddest things to him about attending college here is having his room cleaned, his bed made, his pillows fluffed, and his tea and cookie supply replenished every day. It's like having his mother around, but without all the nagging and judgement.

There's a fulltime cleaning staff at the college, along with someone called a scout who he can go to with any requests or concerns about his room. He's met his scout only once, and very briefly, for he'd been wearing nothing but a towel wrapped around his waist at the time. With a swift knock she entered, sized him up, and then quietly shut the door again. He'd had to tell her by shouting through the door that yes, he was very happy with his room, and that yes, Earl Grey was a perfectly fine tea.

He's just sitting down to organize his books, rather than actually read them, when he hears a knock at the door.

"It's open!"

Anders sidles into the room in another of his T-shirt-under-a-blazer ensembles. Carson isn't sure he owns anything other than a T-shirt or a blazer, but the aesthetic works for Anders and his perpetually windswept blonde hair. Carson feels that if Anders's planned career in archaeology doesn't work out, he could easily find a position as a professional chum to Prince Harry.

As Anders leans his lithe frame against the dresser, Carson still can't quite believe Anders wants to be an archaeologist. Anders had defended himself on the matter. "Well, my good man," he said, "it combines two of my favorite things: technology and the dead."

"The what now?"

Anders grinned. "You heard me. I'm really quite morbid, you know, underneath this fair façade."

Carson concedes there's a sort of glamour to archaeologists—at least successful archaeologists—with the ritzy museum unveilings and splashy *National Geographic* centerfolds. But to reach such heights, they had to shift through a considerable amount of dirt. He looks Anders up and down and decides that no matter what, his roommate would somehow make rolling around in the dirt glamourous in a T-shirt and blazer.

"A few of us were going to go to Fourth Quad," Anders says. "Interested?"

Carson knows his mother would have a heart attack if she knew there's a bar not only on college grounds, but almost directly below him, in the basement of his dormitory. Named Fourth Quad as a sort of joke, since Jesus College has three quadrangles, Fourth Quad services all the student body of age. Which, in England, is eighteen. He can almost hear his mother's heart palpitations.

"Yeah, of course," he says, finding the prospect of not sitting in his room alone tonight nothing short of thrilling. "What time?"

Anders shrugs one shoulder. "Nine-ish, I'd say."

"Sounds great."

After exchanging pleasantries about their first week, Anders pulls himself from the dresser and heads for his own room.

In the ensuing silence, Carson decides, with three-and-a-half hours to spare before starting the evening's festivities, he should try to get *something* done. He flicks open his laptop and opens a blank Word document. The cursor blinks at him menacingly, but he stares it down, determined to put something to virtual paper. He attributes not being able to write anything at all to a frenzied first week. It's the longest stretch he's ever gone without writing since he first started at age eight. After reading somewhere that Hemingway wrote every morning, Carson had dutifully followed in those literary footsteps, even if he only filled a page with nonsense. He often wrote in the evening, despite Hemingway's words of wisdom, finding it a release, an escape from the everyday, a chance to explore the fantastic unknown.

Carson sighs as the cursor continues to blink, daring him to add something to his already enormous *Writings, Musings, Etc.* file. Between doing homework, memorizing the local maps and topography, and trying not to collapse on his bed from the weight of it all, he just can't seem to force words out onto the page. So he gives up.

And decides instead to read the words of others.

Cracking open *The Iliad*, he rifles through the pages until they finally settle on the first chapter heading. He sighs again.

Four chapters in, his head lolls onto the desk. Scooting across the floor in his swivel chair, he goes through the motions of making tea as he munches on one of the individually packaged cookies. He'll need caffeine in his system if he's already nodding off at 7:30.

Finally, 8:50 rolls around, and Carson happily abandons Homer and the small pile of cookie wrappers and tea bags. He changes his shirt, combs his brown hair, happy that it's being reasonable tonight, and with an excited gait crosses the small anteroom to Anders's door.

Entering after hearing Anders call him to come in, Carson leans against the doorframe, watching

Anders discard one blazer and pick up another. What has to be his whole collection is strewn about the room already, decorating the bed, chairs, and floor, but Carson supposes wrinkled clothing is in these days.

After rolling up the sleeves to his mid-forearm, Anders turns with a grand gesture. "And we're off!"

He leads the way out of their room, and as Carson swipes the card key through the reader to lock up, Anders knocks on the door across the hall.

Carson turns at hearing Anneliese's muffled voice calling, "Coming!" A flicker of happiness runs through him, and he hopes Anneliese is coming too.

"We've come to collect you," Anders says when she opens the door.

Anneliese raises her fair eyebrows in surprise, and her eyes flick over Anders's shoulder to Carson.

From out of one of the rooms breezes Anneliese's roommate, a tall girl, almost as tall as he and Anders, with perfectly straight hair, lips parted in a smirk, and diamond earrings that shimmer as if they're real.

"True ladies aren't *collected,*" she says with playful eyes and a perfectly arched brow. "We're escorted."

It's Carson's turn to raise his eyebrows when Anders dips in a mock bow, extending his arm toward the end of the hallway. Anneliese's roommate floats past Carson on a cloud of vanilla scent and laughter, batting Anders's shoulder and letting him lead her, hand on the small of her back, down the hall.

Anneliese meets Carson's bemused look and they share an awkward smile. He waits for her to lock up and then walks with her up the hall, hands clasped behind his back.

"That's Vivien," she says. "But everyone seems to call her Vivi. At least, Anders does."

"You've already met him, then?"

Anneliese looks up at him with laughing eyes. "Carson, *everyone's* met Anders."

She's proven right when, descending the stone steps into the third quadrangle, he's led through a dizzying amount of introductions. There's Niall from next door who Anders assures everyone will be the next Prime Minister. There's Jordan, who's going out for the polo team with Anders. There's Gilly, who went to the same primary school with Anders, and at least four others with some connection to Anders.

Carson's barely through the last handshake when Anders calls for their merry little band to descend into Fourth Quad.

A dimly lit, slightly winding stone staircase deposits them in front of a rather grand wood door boasting a window embossed with a snowy white scroll. Jordan pushes open the door, and the sound and warmth of their fellow college students hits Carson square in the face.

Fourth Quad is a low-ceilinged, whitewashed, narrow bar set with cozy green booths separated by white plaster columns. Off to the right sits a small wooden bar with evenly spaced cushioned stools stationed in front. What looks like an older student-bartender stands behind it, already administering pints of beer. A Michael Jackson song blares from the center of the bar, where a modern jukebox is mounted on one of the columns. Ornate frames hang about the walls, displaying past champion rowing, soccer, rugby, cricket, and polo teams.

Anders's smile carves out a space for their swollen ranks in the middle of the bar. Squished between Anneliese and Niall, Carson carefully puts his hands, fingers intertwined to make one big fist, on the table so that his shoulders angle in, making more room for Anneliese. For her part, Anneliese nips at her thumbnail, and he realizes from the remnants of nail polish near her cuticles that she still bites her nails.

A sort of excited buzzing takes over, and Carson is happy for something to do with his hands when Anders starts collecting pound notes for drinks.

"And what'll it be for our friends from across the pond?" he asks, winking at Anneliese.

"Surprise us," Carson says.

Anders blesses them with a wicked look before

turning with square, determined shoulders toward the bar, taking Vivi with him.

Gilly leans across the table toward Carson and Anneliese so that they can hear her when she says, "How's it been for you this week?" She pushes a hunk of red hair behind her ear, which, like most of her face, is dotted with dark freckles.

Lacing his fingers together again, Carson says, "So far so good. Haven't been mowed down by a car yet."

"Oh, yes, that's right," she says with a smile that dimples her face. "You drive on the other side."

Jordan swings around in his seat next to Gilly at the mention of driving and dwarfs her with his broad shoulders as he too leans toward them. "Alright then, let's find out. I have a question that only an American can answer, and it's of the utmost importance."

Carson grins. "Shoot."

Jordan blinks at him.

Blushing, Carson says, "Go for it."

"Do you Americans really get taken to school in those yellow buses or is that all Hollywood?"

Carson looks between Jordan and another boy and realizes he's to settle a bet. "They're real," he says.

Jordan flings his arms in the air, nearly knocking into Anders and Vivi who are back with two pitchers and three glasses.

"Careful, mate!" Anders chides. "There's some use crying over spilled stout."

Vivi places two of the glasses in front of Carson and Anneliese. It's a bubbly, amber-colored drink with a kebab of fruit and mint leaves levered against the side of the glass.

"Thought we should welcome you with some Pimm's," Vivi says.

Carson takes a sip. It goes down like a minty, spiked Arnold Palmer. It fills his stomach with warmth that radiates out, making him smile. He raises his glass toward Anders, and his roommate nods.

Anders raises his own pint of whatever stout came from the pitcher and says, "We'll work you up to this, mate! All respectable university students live on pints."

"I think we should be offended," he says to Anneliese, who's munching on her fruit kebab.

"I don't mind—this's heavenly."

"Fruity drinks for you, then?"

"Forever and always." She grins as she sucks down another gulp from the straw, and Carson thinks it's the damn cutest thing he's ever seen.

He turns back at the sound of a big fuss being made over Jordan losing his school bus bet. The winner of the bet lays a heavy hand on Jordan's shoulder and says, "It's time to pay up, mate."

Pulling his lower lip down with a finger into an over-exaggerated pout, Jordan gets up with a dramatic sigh and heads for the jukebox. Their group turns to watch as he scrolls through the selections. When he finds something, he slips a twenty-five pence coin into the box and returns to them, ears reddening as a Spice Girls number begins to play.

Anders points a finger at Jordan as he sits back down and begins nursing his pint. "You make a brave show, mate, but I know for a fact you've waxed downright rhapsodic about them before."

For the next twenty minutes, Jordan defends his honor and taste in music, as the jukebox becomes the focal point of the bar. Carson hears a menagerie of pop music from the past three decades, and grins from ear to ear when the whole bar stops to sing along to "Don't Stop Believin'."

When Carson sees Nathan across the bar, he waves the other boy over and makes introductions. Nathan slips easily into their already large group, he and Anders having a less-than-sober conversation about some dig going on in Macedonia.

The conversation eventually morphs into a loud game of Never Have I Ever, where the lowering of fingers reveals that Niall paid for someone to buy him alcohol while underage, Jordan is part of the mile high club, Nathan caught his parents making another sibling, and that Carson and Gilly are the only two of their group still virgins. He's only mildly ashamed to admit it, but what he finds most surprising is that Anneliese isn't.

He isn't given much time to think on it, because when his Pimm's is finished, Anders bestows a pint from the second round of stout. It sits heavy in his stomach, not unpleasantly, and the hoppy taste tickles his nose.

Maybe it's because he's heady on English brews that he's so easily coaxed into a rather vicious battle of *Mario Kart* with Niall and Jordan in the back room of the bar, where, in front of a set of plush, worn couches, is an old-school Nintendo along with an Xbox. Claiming the couches and gaming consoles, their group trickles into the back room one-by-one, drinks in hand, as their noise and wagers mount with each lap. When Carson loses a second time on the infamous Rainbow Road, he throws up his hands in defeat and surrenders his controller to Gilly.

"Have you come to show us how it's done, then?" Jordan says to her with a grin too wide for anyone sober.

"You bet your ass."

Carson slumps back onto the couch, leisurely resting his elbow on the arm, but carefully angling the other so that it isn't quite touching Anneliese. He watches, over the last of his pint, as Gilly soundly beats Jordan. When she wins, his gaze slides over to Anneliese.

Her rather bleary eyes meet his, and Carson realizes she must be on her fourth or fifth Pimm's.

"You okay?"

"Mmhmm," she mumbles. Her head leans onto his shoulder with a contented sigh. "Peachy."

He laughs once. "Probably the one fruit that *isn't* in a Pimm's."

"I like fruit salad."

They sit like that for a long moment, Carson liking the feel of her soft hair brushing his cheek.

"Carson?"

"Yeah?"

But she's asleep.

After two weeks of consistent interaction with Anders's congealing friend group, Carson feels confident he can put a name to every face and tell a third party how they know Anders. They're a lively bunch, and there's always somewhere to go on a Friday night.

Clasping his hands within his warm jacket pockets, Carson forms the caboose of their party train. He's a little disoriented, the twilight bus ride out into the suburbs making his sense of direction give him the slip.

Anders looks back for him in the open doorway. When Carson comes up beside him, Anders lays a lazy arm across his shoulders and says, "Beats the pubs sometimes, this does."

Carson isn't quite convinced as he walks into an already crowded house party. Well, flat party, to be more accurate. He can't help but worry about the blaring noise and hopes the upstairs neighbors are forgiving.

He wishes he could've told Anders no this time, since a rare spell of creativity washed over him after dinner and he felt inclined to write. But Anders had knocked on his door to inform him that the group was headed out in an hour for a party hosted by the polo team captain. Not wanting to be left out, as if his membership would be revoked without consistent participation with the group, Carson faked a smile and confirmed the meeting time. So now here he stands, Anders's hand on his shoulder, trying to convince himself that all this will serve a very important literary purpose later on down the writing road.

The first thing that hits him, after the noise of

course, is the heat. A weary-looking coat rack supports dozens of coats and jackets, many of which have slumped onto the linoleum floor. He waits for Anders to shrug out of his overcoat and roll up the sleeves of his casual linen blazer.

Anders flashes him a devilish grin and says, "Now, I have it on good authority you Americans are wicked at beer pong. Fancy a little transatlantic rivalry? National pride and all."

Despite his protests that he probably isn't the best ambassador for beer pong, Carson's wheeled further into the party as Anders searches for the others. They find Nathan, Jordan, Vivi, and Anneliese watching a beer pong tourney already in heated progress.

"We'll take the table next, Clark," Anders says, distracting the young man about to take a shot.

Clark gives Anders an affectionately ugly glare and shoots without looking, plunking it into the awaiting cup. His partner claps his back animatedly as his opponents across the table suck down the cup of lukewarm beer.

As Anders chats with Clark, no doubt securing their rights to the table next, Jordan and Vivi disappear for a moment through a swinging door that seems to lead to a bright kitchen. They return with mismatched cups full of wine.

“Not Bordeaux, but it’ll do,” Vivi says, clinking glasses with Anneliese.

Carson grins into his cup, still delightfully unsure if Vivi’s serious when she says such things. He leans down to whisper to Anneliese, confident he won’t be overheard in the boisterous room.

“Do you think she’s ever actually had Bordeaux?” Carson asks, more curious than accusing.

Anneliese’s nose wrinkles as she tries not to smile. “Probably. Her parents are disgustingly rich. They’ve got a summer home somewhere south that looks like one of the colleges.”

“As if I didn’t feel poor enough,” Carson says

through another sip of wine. Bordeaux or no, it's pretty decent. For bitter grape juice.

"Her dad's in the publishing industry. Owns a couple imprints. And her mother's an author."

"Oh yeah? Anything I might've read?"

"Probably not." She bats her eyelashes at him. "Nothing with dragons."

He puts his hand on his chest and pulls a face, as if she'd sent an arrow straight through his heart.

Anders pops up in front of them and, with another of his signature disarming grins, relieves them of their cups and pushes them to one side of the table.

"Oh, no, I don't think—" Carson tries.

"No protests, please. National pride and all."

Deciding Anders must've been watching soccer earlier—he only feels "national pride" during and directly after watching soccer—Carson asks Anneliese, "Should we let them win?"

"It shouldn't be hard—I'm terrible," she admits.

She sells herself short, and Carson feels nothing

less than national pride as each of her shots finds its way into one of Anders's and Jordan's cups. He doesn't think much of it when she drinks each of the cups Anders or Jordan manages to land, since she seems to get better with each cup she's obligated to drink. When the game ends and they've won, Carson happily bows away so that everyone can laud Anneliese's Herculean show.

Anders is dipping in a mock bow when Carson finally reaches the wall and slumps against it. When he's called back for another round, Carson does his best to gracefully wriggle free of the call to arms. None of the other boys in the room seem disappointed, Nathan stepping up to fill his spot next to Anneliese with a pleased smile.

Carson's happy to have at least one contribution to Anders's large group with Nathan, but now his heart prickles seeing his mistake. Even as the second round, and then another, goes by, he can't make himself return to claim the spot on her team. She's laughing and smiling and it's nice to look at.

But Carson knows he isn't the only one looking and suddenly needs to leave the room.

He isn't quick enough, however, and watches with a sort of choked feeling as Anneliese and Nathan head into the kitchen, his hand on the small of her back. Carson has a sore spot in his chest thinking of the couple times he and Anneliese have gotten to hang out—a few walks, another stop to a café for coffee, one chat in his room with tea and cookies. She's always reserved, her smiles rare. But here, at a party, she's lively, even bubbly, and Carson glimpses the happy person she used to be. What, then, does that mean for when they're together alone? Why is she awkward around him but smiling at Nathan?

Deciding he has a headache blooming beneath his right eye, Carson determines to leave as he sips again from the wine cup, recently refilled by Vivi. He peers at his friends over the rim of the cup. He sees smiles and ruddy cheeks and knows he's free to go.

Losing himself in the crowd, he meanders his way through the house, not really having an end goal. He would think more about how different flats and townhomes are compared to the average two-storied American house if he didn't have to constantly dodge bodies. He smiles; he waves to a few people he knows; he gets pushed up against a baluster. Looking up, he sees a narrow staircase and wonders if it'd be quieter up there.

As he hops up the stairs, he avoids as many intertwined couples as he can. They're hard to look away from, but he does his best, cheeks burning.

The stairs lead to a narrow corridor with two doors on each side. It's cooler up here and smells faintly of pine-scented candles and weed. One couple stumbles into the first door on the left and disappears from sight. Carson tries his luck with the second door on the right. He opens it a crack, revealing a cool, dark bedroom.

Sucking in a relieved breath, Carson takes a

hesitant step into the bedroom. He isn't usually one to stray into a bedroom uninvited, but he just wants to disappear for a while. He'd play a few games on his phone, give them about an hour, then go check on everyone. Maybe by then Anneliese will have broken free of Nathan.

A small intake of breath makes him jump back into the wall. A girl sits on the bed, her dark hair and large eyes framed eerily in the blue light of her phone.

"Oh, erm, s-sorry I didn't think—"

"It's alright," she says with an easy smile. She leans toward a nightstand and flicks on a lamp.

Dim light splashes onto her corner of the room and casts him in shadows. She's wearing a green button-up shirt tucked into a black skirt. Her legs are pulled up under her and clad in black tights; her leather Oxford shoes lay primly on the ground.

"Are you hiding out too?" she asks.

His throat works trying to form words, but he nearly chokes.

"You're in my English class, I think."

Now it's his brain's turn to choke. Carson takes a breath, forcing himself to think, to place her face. It takes a moment, but yes, he remembers her. Always toward the front of the class. Always in a button-up shirt, putting the rest of them to shame.

Finally, he says, "Yeah."

She gives him an amused grin, and he realizes how sheepish he must look.

Running his hands along his hips, he says, "I didn't mean to barge in. I can leave."

She waves a hand. "Whatever you'd like. This isn't my room."

"Do you know whose it is?"

She shakes her head of curly brown hair. "No idea whose flat it is, even."

He grins at that. "May I?"

"Please."

Sitting down cross-legged on the floor a few feet from the bed, he tries not to look as awkward as he feels while he turns his phone over in his clammy hands.

"Oh, I'm Mandy by the way," she says, reaching a hand toward him.

He lifts himself on a knee and takes the hand. It's so much smaller than his. "Carson."

"Sorry," she says with a blushing smile, "I should have done that before you sat."

He shrugs as he sits again. He wonders how he hadn't noticed how cute she was before. Probably because she's always at the front when he's always at the back. From the back he couldn't tell how sharp her dark eyes are, though they crinkle at the corners, nor how her mouth seems perpetually on the verge of a grin.

"You're American."

He nods. "You're British."

"I'm English," she corrects.

"Ah, yes, sorry."

The edges of her mouth twitch up. "You could

get yourself in real trouble, mixing us up. You're lucky I wasn't a Scot."

"Fair enough," he says.

"Where in the States are you from?"

"California," he says, rapidly feeling more at ease.

"Do you surf much?"

It's his turn to laugh now. "Never done it in my life."

"Have you seen many celebrities?"

"Not one."

She makes a face at him. "Are you sure you live in California then?"

"Yes—northern California. In the mountains."

She smiles down at him and he smiles back at her. Carson hates to admit that Anders was right; sometimes parties are better than pubs.

And as if thinking about Anders summoned him, none other than his roommate comes barreling through the door, a giggling Vivi right behind him.

"Ope, taken," Anders says with bleary eyes, which quickly focus on Carson. "There you are, mate!" Next he looks over at Mandy sitting on the bed. She's moved back against the wall as far as she can.

Anders dons a lopsided smirk and tells Carson, "It works best if you're *both* on the bed, y'know."

"Crazy night?"

Carson raises his head from his palm. He regrets it instantly, a searing pain throbbing along his hairline as he does.

The girl from last Friday's party, the girl who always sits in the front of his English class, Mandy, is smiling at him, having slipped onto the bench beside him.

"It's nice to see you in real lighting," Mandy says, though she blushes a little once she has.

He runs a hand through his hair, hoping it isn't as bad as he imagines. "I'm not so sure about that."

She looks him up and down, and Carson holds

his breath. "You look a little worse for wear," she admits.

"I *feel* a little worse for wear," he groans, resting half his face in his hand, his eyelids drooping.

She grins, her eyes crinkling around the edges. She gets up and disappears from the dining hall, returning quickly with a steaming mug of something. Placing the black coffee in front of him, she looks at him expectantly. "Drink up."

He wrinkles his nose, unenthused at the prospect of instant coffee. "It's poison like that," he says.

"Oh, don't be a baby," she says with a smile as she swings her legs over the bench again and begins stirring her bowl of Irish stew. She smells like cinnamon.

"But it's six o'clock."

"It'll help, I promise. I wouldn't subject anyone to black coffee if I didn't think it'd help."

Carson stirs it, watching steam slowly curl from the brown surface. "So it's true coffee's a hangover cure?"

"It's worked for me before," she says before biting into a buttered slab of bread. "At least for all beer-related hangovers."

He takes an obedient sip. "I suppose I *should* like it like this."

"Why?"

He blinks, only then realizing he'd said that aloud. Blushing, Carson says, "Because I want to be a writer."

A grin overcomes her face, and she tosses her mane of short brown curls over to one side of her head. "Oh, yeah? That's exciting, to find a fellow writer."

"You too?"

"Mmhmm. I haven't been doing it for very long, but I love it already. What do you like to write?"

He shrugs, wishing that his headache would go away long enough for him to seem like a nice, sane person to this cute, smiling writer sitting next to him. Nobody has ever brought him a hangover cure before.

"A little of everything, I guess. I think the most fun thing is male mid-life crises."

"A gold mine, that," she agrees. Her look turns rueful, and she cocks an eyebrow. "Having one yourself?"

"I hope not—I'll be dead before I'm forty if I am. What about you? Any favorite genre?"

"I'm always a fan of a murder mystery, though I'm still figuring out how to write one. I have to have the crime solved before I even start writing. I'm afraid I'm always being too obvious with my clues."

"Well, it can't be any worse than Nancy Drew."

He's stunned by how fast her face slips and horrified when she says, "Nancy Drew was my childhood hero."

"Oh, I'm sorry, I—"

She giggles. "I'm kidding, I'm kidding!"

Despite glowering at her as his head slips back into his hand, he smiles. "Haven't you heard not to kick a man while he's down?"

She continues laughing to herself as she spoons another piece of stewed meat into her mouth, her eyes dancing. "You know what we should do," she says, suddenly excited and only halfway done chewing. "We should start a writing club or something. I checked and they don't have one already."

"Like a workshop?"

"I think it could be fun, having informal advice from peers."

He nods then winces. "That sounds great."

"Marvelous! I'm not sure if we'd need a professor overseeing it, but I don't mind doing the legwork to get it started."

"We'd probably need somewhere to meet, but if we can't get a classroom, there's always the common room, or even a pub."

She leans forward on a wave of enthusiasm and says, "There's the pub where the Inklings met—you know, Tolkien, C.S. Lewis, all of them."

"Eagle and Something, isn't it?"

Mandy nods, curls bouncing. "Eagle and Child.

They met there all the time. Perhaps it'd be fitting to have it there."

"I've been meaning to go."

"Me too! Now we've got an excuse."

They share a smile.

"Maybe we should go take a look this weekend, make sure it's big enough for a group of us."

"I'd like that. Maybe . . . "—his heart misses a beat—"we can do some other touristy things while we're at it."

He sits there on the bench, all at once too hot and too cold. Carson can't quite believe the words came out of his mouth, but then, he hasn't had a friend to go with yet. All the outings he goes on with Anders and his group are to pubs, and unfortunately the Eagle and Child hasn't been one of them. Anneliese is kept busy with her introductory science and chemistry courses, and his class acquaintances are coming along slower than anticipated.

"Yeah," she says with a smile. "That'd be great. I've got a whole checklist going, but I haven't gotten to strike anything out since classes started. We can make a day of it. Do you have a local mobile?"

"Yeah, but I can't for the life of me ever remember the number."

She motions him to hand over the phone, and quickly types away, handing it back to him with the new entry: *Mandy Aarons.*

"We probably shouldn't go punting, though. I can't be trusted not to tip any boat I'm in."

"Your loss—I practically grew up in a canoe."

"A shame, that. Canoeing when you could have been celebrity-watching." Checking her phone for the time, Mandy pushes her bowl back and stands. "It's the witching hour, I'm afraid."

"I'll see you in class tomorrow?"

She nods. "Especially if you sit in the front for once." And then she's away, half her face buried in a massive, lumpy, knit scarf.

Carson does his best to eat the rest of his stew through his smile. The coffee and stew don't mix well, however, and he decides to drink up the coffee before finally leaving the dining hall himself. He usually spends as long as he can in the dining hall; it's his favorite place on campus. Daily meals are served in the ancient hall, long rows of student tables and benches bearing pristine white china and folded napkins, with the three golden stags of Jesus College emblazoned on the face, all leading toward a raised dais with the professors' table á la Harry Potter. Watching over them is an authentic portrait of Queen Elizabeth I, founder of the college, along with other notable Jesus alumni, including, to Carson's bemused delight, the real Lawrence of Arabia. Carson's always been a slow eater, but when he eats here, he stalls so that he can stay longer.

But his head's throbbing, and he can't guarantee he won't fall asleep in his half-finished stew. Jamming his hands into his pockets to keep them from the crisp October night air, Carson heads back to his dorm.

The unfamiliar sound hits him just after the front door shuts behind him. It's a moaning interspersed with soft, rhythmic creaks. His cheeks blazing, Carson hurriedly unlocks his room, his fingers fumbling, and the door can't close quickly enough. But he can hear it in here too, as Anders's tempo seems to have upped.

He stands in the middle of his room, his fists clenching and unclenching. It wouldn't be as much of a problem if he hadn't lost his only set of headphones just this weekend. His head throbs too much to go out searching for a new pair, and besides, he doesn't know anywhere that would be open right now that would sell them.

Opting to collapse on his bed, Carson huddles against the wall, his head buried beneath his two pillows. The moaning is gone, but the thumping is still there. His insides squirm as the pulsing in his head starts to keep rhythm with Anders and, he assumes, Vivi. He wills himself to go to sleep, but his headache only worsens under the pressure of the pillows and his hand that keeps them balanced squarely over his ear.

With a sigh, Carson collects his laptop and flees the room for the quiet of the emergency staircase at the end of the hall.

Sitting on the top step, Carson gently leans his head against the wall, the cool of it feeling nice against his throbbing temple. He tries his best to push his embarrassment down, to remind himself that it is all part of the college experience. With a little time and perspective, who knows? He could turn this evening into an award-winning short story.

He's been reading the same two lines from *Beowulf* for twenty minutes when the phone rings. A sort of odd sensation settles in the pit of his stomach and his fingers tingle when he checks the caller ID.

"Hi, Mom," he says.

"Oh, Carson! It's so good to hear your voice!"

He closes his heavy eyelids. "You'd think I'd been lost at sea."

His mother clucks at him, tells him to stop teasing, and he smiles.

"How're you, Mom?" He tries hard to keep the fatigue out of his voice.

"Oh, fine. You're sister's down with the flu so I've been playing nurse all week." He didn't need to be told which sister; whenever it was cold season, Amy, without fail, caught whatever was going around, despite being devoted to hand sanitizer. "And Jake thinks he's coming down with it too."

"He just doesn't want to go to school."

"Probably. It's been raining a lot lately. We must've brought it home with us when . . . " She clears her throat. "I'm glad I caught you—you haven't been answering the phone."

"I've been in class," he says. "I printed you out that time chart, the one that shows the time difference, remember?"

"Yes, I'm looking at it right now." He can picture her now, standing with one hand holding the phone, the other on her hip, as she stares at the fridge door where the chart is held on with ABC magnets. "It's almost eleven here, so it's . . . about seven for you?"

"Yup."

"Have you had dinner? You're remembering to eat, aren't you?"

"If anything I'm eating too much."

"Well that can be just as bad. I read an article last week that 'the Freshman Fifteen' is a real thing."

"I can believe it."

"Speaking of eating," she says in one of her famous segues, "I was wondering when you'll be flying back for Thanksgiving. I know schools don't like to let you go very early, but one of us will have to be down there to meet you and then there's . . . "

He lets her go on with her rambling about traffic being murder Thanksgiving week and how she's already put her order in at the grocery store for a twenty-five-pound bird because he's stalling. He doesn't know how to tell her.

"Mom . . . " he says finally. "I won't be there for Thanksgiving."

" . . . What?"

"Thanksgiving isn't an English holiday," he explains. "I'm not getting the time off. But I'll be home for—"

"But we've always been together for Thanksgiving."

"I'm sorry, Mom. There's nothing I can do. I'll have classes all that week."

"Can't you tell them that—?"

"They aren't going to give me special treatment. It's only English holidays we have off here."

"I see." She sniffs, and he can hear the sound of her rummaging through the fridge, probably about to make someone a sandwich even though no one asked, out of habit. "Well then I'd better call the store back, see if they have a twenty-two pound bird, since . . . "

"I'm really sorry. I wish I could be there. But I'll be home for Christmas."

Her voice is distant when she says, "That's good."

He takes a deep breath and lets it out as a sigh.

His eyes feel like they're sinking further into his skull as he closes them.

"I guess I'd better let you go, then," she says finally. "Wouldn't want to eat up all your minutes."

"I'm sorry, Mom," is all he can think to say.

"Me too. But it'll be alright. I'll talk to you soon?"

He makes a noncommittal "Mm," from deep in his throat, tells her he loves her, and then hangs up with a breath of relief. In the haze of pain from his headache, Carson admits to himself that he misses his home, his siblings, his parents. He misses the smell of the lake at sunset, how the night sky explodes with stars once the sun sinks below the mountains. But most of all, he misses knowing what it is he's doing.

Rallying his spirits, he cracks an eye open, determined to read the assigned article comparing imagery in Milton. The blue LED light of his laptop stabs at his eyes, and he swiftly closes it again with a ferocious *thunk.*

Being beheaded would be a merciful alternative to this. He rubs his forehead in rhythmic little circles, concentrating on the movements so hard that he barely hears the footsteps coming up the stairs. Opening one cautious eye, Carson sees Anneliese. He tries to smile a greeting but knows he looks rather pathetic.

"Hey," she says, looking him up and down.

"Hey."

"You alright?"

"I've been better."

"Headache?"

"Mm."

The corners of her mouth seem to want to twitch up in a smile, but she keeps her concerned frown with obvious effort. "I didn't know staircases were the remedy for headaches."

"I wish," he groans. "My room wasn't very peaceful."

"No?"

He remembers at the last minute not to shake his head. "Anders has company."

"But you don't share rooms."

"Yes, but we aren't in the dormitory made out of sturdy medieval stone walls." He shrugs one shoulder. "It's fine, I just didn't . . . "

"Ah," she says, clearing her throat. "I suppose it's Vivi with him."

He opens one eye again. "Yeah?"

"Mmhmm. They're rather into each other, if you hadn't noticed."

"I *had*, which is saying something."

"Yes, you are rather dense sometimes." She says it with a sweet smile, so he isn't the least offended. In fact, he can hear blood rushing in his ears, and it isn't from the headache.

"Well you can come in with me, if you'd like. I have some studying to do, but I can keep the light low."

"That'd be heaven, thanks."

She hops up the last few steps, and Carson

follows her back into the hallway toward her door. Once she's swiped open both doors, she ushers him in. Her room is much like his—narrow twin bed with starched white sheets, which are tangled into a hopeless knot at the foot—heavy green curtains that match the forest-green carpet, tea tray, desk, two chairs. All that's missing is the bay window. Her view is down into the third quadrangle rather than the street like his.

He can't help the grin when he sees the touches of the room that make it Anneliese's. She's just about as messy as he remembers, with clothes and papers strewn about. What looks to be at least three winter coats are hung over the back of her desk chair, heavy wool mixing with sturdy cotton and fake fur. She's replaced the white pillow covers with her own flouncy teal ones with lacy trim, and he's happy to see teal still seems to be her favorite color. It decorates her laptop, her phone cover, and several shades of it are ranged about in a little shrine of nail polish bottles. On the corkboard behind the desk, despite what she said about giving up photography, are a pleasant mix of postcards and photos of Hawaiian beaches, Alaskan glaciers, Indian markets, and Roman ruins.

"Have you been to all these places?" he asks.

She looks up from her desk, which she's discreetly trying to tidy up, and follows his gaze. "Oh, a few. My mom dragged me up to Alaska two years ago, but we didn't get out of Juneau. And I've been to Maui a few times with my dad."

"How is your dad?" he asks. It's the first time she's mentioned him.

Anneliese's father had been a rather accomplished horseman, even went to the Olympics back in the eighties, but a fall during a warmup had cost him much of his mobility. He had to use a cane and hadn't gotten back into the saddle. When the prize money ran dry, so did Mrs. Johansson's affections for her husband, as Carson's mother liked to put it, and they divorced. Anneliese's mother got full custody and the summer home in Tahoe, which she promptly sold. Whatever happened to Mr. Johansson was even more of a mystery to Carson than what happened to Anneliese.

She shrugs. "Fine. Working."

He doesn't press her for more than those two clipped words, but he wishes she'd tell him more. Did she wish she could have gone with him? Was it true that in the nasty divorce battle, the one matter he hadn't fought Mrs. Johansson on was custody of Anneliese?

"So," she says, taking on a forced, breezier tone, "would you like something for the headache?"

"Yeah, if you've got something."

"You want prescription or over-the-counter?" she tosses over her shoulder as she walks out of the room toward the bathroom.

"Um . . . "

She opens one of the small drawers in the bathroom, revealing at least five orange prescription bottles and several other white ones with company logos and medicinal names not found in nature scrawled across the face. He blinks, forgetting her question, pondering why she would have so many.

"I get migraines sometimes," she says.

He looks up from the drawer, but she catches the tail-end of his stare.

Clearing his throat, Carson says, "I don't know. Whichever works fastest I guess."

She nods and then turns back toward the drawer, her shoulders angled so that he can't see the bottles anymore. When she turns back, she lets a blue-and-gray capsule fall into his palm.

"This should do the trick."

Swallowing it dry, Carson gives her an appreciative grin. "Thanks. I'm never good at taking things when I need to."

"I don't believe in being a martyr," she says, leading him back into her room.

She settles herself in her swivel chair as Carson stands in the middle of the room, his hands finding their way into his pockets.

"I don't want to be in your way," he says, suddenly shy.

She waves him off. "I'll just be doing homework."

Slumping into one of the green chairs, Carson leans his head on the back, testing positions until he finds a sweet spot that doesn't aggravate his headache too badly. He closes his eyes and stretches his legs out in front of him comfortably.

"Is that okay?" she asks.

"Mm," he mumbles. "Much better than the stairs."

"I'd hope so."

He listens as she begins to work, her fingers quietly tapping at the keyboard. He means to ask her how she's doing, how classes are, if she thinks her first round of exams will be as bad as he thinks his will be, why she never tried contacting him over the past years, but the medicine starts to kick in. It's stronger than he's used to, and through a fuzzy sort of contentedness, he decides she definitely gave him something prescription. He fades listening to her phone ring, to her saying hurried, sharp words into it.

He's aware he's fallen asleep; he can feel himself stretched out in that chair, can hear Anneliese moving about the room then going to sleep herself, but his head is swimming in pain-free bliss. His dreams are a bit odd, the runny image of Milton sitting down for Thanksgiving making him wonder what all a drug company can pack into one little capsule.

He wakes in what has to be the middle of the night. At first he thinks the crick in his neck must be what woke him, but then he hears something soft, muffled. He holds his breath, listening, and then registers what it is.

With quiet sobs, Anneliese is crying into her pillow.

Carson's heart hammers in his chest, and he thinks she has to hear it. But she sniffles and he hears her shift a little, as if further into the pillow. She cries and he sits there, unsure what to do. And so he clenches and unclenches his fists helplessly, just listening.

Carson pauses reaching for the front door when he hears Anders open his.

"Thought you were in," Anders says, leaning against the doorframe. "A few of us were going out to a pub this afternoon."

"Sorry, I can't this time."

A shadow of a frown crosses Anders's face. "But it's the Manchester match." He looks as if Carson's offended Great Britain as a whole in one fell swoop.

Though he's successfully pretended to care about soccer thus far—only slipping up and calling it *soccer* instead of *football* once—Carson has a more legitimate excuse than lack of interest. "I made plans to go out. I'm sorry—I'll try and catch up with you later though, yeah? Text me where you end up."

Anders nods, seemingly appeased, and Carson makes his escape, the giddy feeling in the center of chest returning.

Mandy is sitting on the wide stone steps in front of the dorm building waiting for him. He hops down, standing beside her.

"Morning," he says, proud of himself for only sounding mildly shy, and extends a hand to help her up.

She takes it and smiles. He can barely see it, though, since the lumpy knit scarf has returned. In the crispness of the October morning, Carson half wishes he had a lumpy scarf of his own.

"I've made up a route that should maximize our touristing," she says.

He grins at her made-up verb. "So where're we going first?"

"I was thinking Christ Church. Today is one of their open weekends."

"Sounds good to me," he says as they start toward Jesus's side entrance which opens onto the narrow, alley-like Ship Street. "Though I should warn you that I'm liable to cry a bit."

Her eyes twinkle at him as they step through the large door onto Ship Street. "Everyone's allowed to be a fangirl when it comes to Harry Potter," she says.

His heart beats quickly in his chest to think that he'll soon be in the dining hall that inspired the Great Hall in the *Harry Potter* movies. Not to mention the staircase a doe-eyed Daniel Radcliffe hopped up before being sorted into Gryffindor.

They emerge onto Turl Street and walk along the high wall of the neighboring Exeter College. Turning onto a narrow lane, Carson smiles involuntarily as they're deposited into a corner of a wide, sunny, cobblestone square. The Radcliffe Camera, the centerpiece of the square, dominates the space. Carson doesn't think he'll ever tire of seeing the giant rotunda, with its yellowy columns and blue dome.

The Camera stands in the center of the square, surrounded by other hallowed buildings. To the north are university buildings including the Bodleian Library, the Clarendon Building, and the Sheldonian Theatre. All students, no matter what college, have access to these buildings, and final exams are taken there as well. Pushing away the thought of exams with haste, Carson turns his head east, to see the delicate gray spires of All Soul's College as they round the other side of the Camera.

Carson and Mandy head south, away from the university buildings toward the Church of St. Mary the Virgin.

"Is climbing the tower on the to-do list?" he asks. He's heard from none other than Rick Steves himself, that the medieval tower offers spectacular views of the heart of the city.

"Definitely," says Mandy, "but they aren't open for that today."

"Rain check, then?"

She gives him a bemused look.

"Some other time?" he amends.

"Oh," she smiles, "yes. Hopefully next weekend is as nice as this one."

Since they can't climb St. Mary's tower and take in what has to be a breathtaking view of the Camera, he contents himself walking down a little lane between the church and another building where a black lamppost stands commandingly in the middle. His mother's guidebook asserted this lamppost had been an inspiration for C.S. Lewis, for he had walked this very path on his way to teach at Magdalen College.

Emerging onto High Street, they duck past Land Rovers, Volvos, and disappointingly modern double-decker buses to dive down another small street.

"Tell me something about America," she says as they walk.

"What would you like to know?"

She considers. "How many states have you been to?"

"Six, including Washington, D.C."

She frowns. "What's that mean?"

"Washington isn't part of any state. It's like a city-state."

"Oh, yes, I see. Then what others have you been to?" She holds up two fingers, saying they are for California and D.C.

"Nevada," she holds up another finger, "Oregon, Hawaii, and New York."

Mandy makes a happy sound in her throat at the mention of Hawaii. "Now *that's* on the to-do list," she says.

"It rains there a lot too. It'd feel like home for you." He gets a playful scowl for that. "Though, honestly the rain's about seventy degrees there—much nicer."

She opens then closes her mouth before saying, "Ah. Fahrenheit."

He blushes. "Yeah."

He's spared trying to convert Fahrenheit to Celsius as they come upon the main gate to Christ Church College. The four-storied stone façade greets them with majesty. Pointed arches shelter cased windows, some with stone balconies, as startlingly green ivy sprawls up to the second story. Two levels of bay windows hang above the great wooden doors, thrown open on their iron hinges. They pass through these into a cool stone gallery running along all four sides of an open-air quadrangle, and Carson realizes he's looking at another piece of architecture the *Harry Potter* movies borrowed from Christ Church.

They aren't the only tourists; he and Mandy soon fall into step with about a half-dozen other people, two of whom also look like fellow students from another college, and a family of what Carson assumes, after catching snatches of their conversation, are Germans. There are no tour guides to give them well-placed factoids as they meander further into the college, but Mandy gets her hands on a brochure as they make their way up a smooth staircase. When they make a turn and head up another flight of wide, shallow steps, a little thrill goes through Carson, and he imagines what it would be like to mount these steps with a looming Dame Maggie Smith watching over him.

He and Mandy exchange giddy looks as they make their way into an anteroom filled with gilt-framed portraits of notable Christ Church alumni. Past this room, the dining hall spreads out before them in Tudor magnificence. Heavy wooden walls, laden with more portraits including Prime Ministers and monarchs, give way to stone with sloping, angular windows that let shafts of light slant into the room before arching up into a dark wood ceiling. The ceiling is made up of ridged timbers, giving it the look of the inside of a ship's hull. Three long tables run down the length of the Great Hall.

The front of the Great Hall is almost completely engulfed in glare from an ornate medieval window. It lets in so much light that he can barely make out the large portraits hung there until almost upon them. Set above the professors' table are the Tudors themselves, most prominently Henry VIII, with his daughter Elizabeth on his right.

They make a U-turn to walk back down the length of the hall, and Carson strolls past other famous faces, including John Locke and Lewis Carroll. The light pouring in from the medieval window illuminates the rest of the hall in a halo of blue light and makes the feeble yellow light from the anachronistic table lamps ranged about look pathetically modern.

When his head swings over to look at Mandy, he sees she's wearing the same expression. They share a smile as they stand just beyond the threshold of the doors, catching one last long look at the Great Hall.

"I'd say we should have another turn if he didn't look so grumpy." She nods at the hook-nosed, heavy-lidded attendant in black livery standing guard a few steps away from them on the other side of the threshold.

"I'm sure he's seen worse than us."

"I suppose watching adults sobbing like children can get old after a while," she says.

So they hop back down the staircase, both of them stopping for a moment to snap a rare picture of the stairs tourist-free, and wander out into the main quad. Christ Church's main quad looks as if it could fit all of Jesus College inside it, two towers looming over either side like stony sentries. Delicate fountains decorate the immaculate lawn, and a golden clock ticks off the time on the opposite tower.

With a glance at the brochure, Mandy leads them toward the bell tower. When they've made it back out onto the street, Mandy turns back, craning her head to take in the tower's height.

"Why can't we all have bell towers?"

He chuckles and she turns to smile at him.

"Onwards?"

"Onwards," he agrees.

After a mandatory visit to an ice cream shop, they continue their trek up the slight incline of the road, finally coming to a wide intersection. Cornmarket spreads out before them on the other side. They pause on their way to give St. Michael a thorough look but don't go in on account of their sticky, melting snacks.

"What part of England are you from?" he asks between mouthfuls of mint chocolate chip.

"Can you guess?" She arches an eyebrow and takes a defiant bite of rocky road.

He narrows his eyes in mock appraisal. "Not north."

She nods. "Very good."

"So . . . south?"

She laughs and has mercy on him. "I'm from Bath. My parents run a little bed and breakfast there, for the tourists."

"Oh, wow, really? I'll bet you could tell stories."

"Well I certainly know my way around nineteenth-century plumbing, if that's what you mean," she says with a rueful look.

"Your house is nineteenth century?"

"Yes. Early Victorian. The records Mum found put it at about 1840." She stops and stares at his amused bafflement. "What?"

He shakes his head. "It's just amazing how old everything is here."

"1840 isn't *terribly* old."

"California wasn't even a state in 1840."

"Really?"

He nods. "I'm pretty sure Jesus College is older than the U.S., too."

"I guess we just don't really think about it that much." She shrugs. "We just accept we've got a terrible amount of history and resign ourselves to memorizing the monarchs, from Alfred to Elizabeth."

"And here I thought memorizing a few presidents was bad."

"They make you memorize them too?"

"Mm-hmm. Though it usually gets fuzzy between Lincoln and Roosevelt."

Tossing their empty, albeit milky, cups away, Carson finds Mandy has deftly led them to the front of the Ashmolean Museum. Colorful banners advertise the latest exhibits as they pass under the tall Greco-Roman porch into a cool, gray interior. Turning to his immediate left, antiquity smacks him across the face.

Mandy guides him to the first long hall, displaying a group of marble and plaster busts and statues. The museum deftly guides them through history, beginning with Greek statuary then meandering to Egyptian sarcophagi. He smiles as he watches Mandy, out of the corner of his eye, trying to take a panorama picture of everything with a decidedly determined glint in her eyes.

He's struck when he sees tall, bronze Roman statues.

"It's a shame they're not the originals," he says, almost hushed. How else does one talk about something ancient?—at least, fake ancient.

"Have to go to Rome for that, I'd think. But all the best stolen things are at the British Museum in London," she says with a devilish smile that tells him she hasn't a qualm about Britain housing the treasures of the rest of the world.

Her first words are the ones that stick with him, however, as they mount a flight of stairs and start going through the Ashmolean's Asian art collection. As he lets his eyes wander over many fine examples of Chinese porcelain, his thoughts are on those words: Go to Rome. If only. He frowns. Well, he's a hell of a lot closer than he would be in Tahoe—he's already made the lion's share of the journey. It couldn't be hard, he reasons, to steal away to another European nation for a day or two, right? He'd probably need a bit longer than a weekend, though. His thoughts turn sour over an original Stradivarius violin when he thinks of how his mother would never forgive him for not going back home on a long-enough holiday.

Mandy doesn't let him pout for long, though. He smiles, amused and baffled, at her looking dumbfounded at an oil painting of a somberly dressed, middle-aged Renaissance woman. Mandy's eyes, the size of saucers, turn to him.

"It's a real Rembrandt," she whispers.

His eyebrows shoot up, and together they take an inordinate amount of pictures, just short of telling Rembrandt's mother to "Work it."

He squints in the afternoon light when they finally emerge, and he can't quite believe it's stayed nice for so long. He's become nothing short of suspicious of English weather.

Stretching out his shoulders, he says, "I think we've earned lunch."

Mandy nods heartily and points back out toward the road. It's a short walk up the street to the Eagle and Child pub. Passing through the hallowed door, Carson feels like he's entering a church, no matter how pretentiously literary it might be to think it. The pub is narrow, cozy, floor-to-ceiling a dark, lacquered wood. A woman behind the bar smiles at them, inclining her head at an empty table for two in a niche across from the bar.

Carson takes only a minute to look at the menu, seeing it's the same as many of the other old pubs in town, and instead looks about. He's heard Tolkien and the Inklings had a favorite booth, toward the front, and wonders if there's a mile-long waitlist to sit there. If there isn't, there should be.

"Know what you want?"

He nods and heads with Mandy up to the bar. He still isn't used to ordering at the bar, even for meals—though it does virtually eliminate the problem of splitting the check. When this passes through his head, he's quick to slap a large enough pound note on the bar once he's ordered after Mandy so that he pays for lunch.

"You didn't have to," she says as they walk back to their niche.

"You did all the research. We've made impeccable time today thanks to you."

She still pulls a face. "I'll get the next one, yes?"

A warm, fuzzy feeling expands in his stomach as he nods.

For a moment they sit in silence, each looking again at the pub. Mandy stands and disappears for a quick minute and then returns.

"There are some larger tables in the back. I think this'd be perfect for a workshop."

"Wouldn't it be crazy if we all wrote masterpieces like them?"

A little dimple appears in her left cheek when she smiles. "Hopefully they'd give us a decent group name."

"It's pretty hard to top 'the Inklings,' though."

"Very true."

When the bartender brings over their pints, Mandy clinks hers against his. "To writing masterpieces."

Collecting his papers, still warm from the printer, Carson logs off and exits the cavernous computer lab. Three weeks after his initial scouting mission with Mandy and two workshops in, he's a little ashamed that another submission will be an old piece, but he still hasn't broken through his writer's block, no matter how many times he stares down that damn cursor.

Checking his watch, he realizes how close it is to the meeting time and hurries up the stairs to his dorm. Placing the multiple copies of the short story into a folder, he rounds up a few more effects before filling and shouldering his backpack. He's locking up his front door when he hears Anneliese say his name.

He turns and grins. “Hey.”

“Hi.” She looks at his backpack. “I didn’t think you had class this late.”

“I don’t—I’m headed to a writing workshop with a few people from my English class.”

“So you’re not coming with us?”

He blinks. He can’t remember Anders saying anything about a Manchester United game, but then, he hasn’t seen much of Anders lately. Night is about the only time of day their schedules match up, and since he hasn’t been going out, he can only assume from the occasional muffled flush from the bathroom that Anders is still alive.

There’s been too much to do to go out, with the first round of exams come and gone and the next looming dead ahead just before winter break. He’s been trying to salvage his reading list, but as he tries to play catch-up while simultaneously doing the current assignments, he feels himself sinking further.

He atones for this by not going out, by staying in his room and reading, but there's still a maddening pile of books sitting on his desk.

That, and there have been dates with Mandy. His stomach feels funny just thinking her name. The past two weekends they've gone out and checked more off of her tourist to-do list. They finally climbed St. Mary's tower, and he's now the proud owner of several sweeping panoramas of the steepled Oxford skyline. They wandered through the Natural History Museum, full of dinosaurs, fossils, and Darwin's own stuffed dodo. They've gone reverently into the Bodleian to see its core medieval library; to the Bridge of Sighs—which certainly earned one from both Carson and Mandy—a beautiful covered stone bridge standing two stories up and modeled after something similar in Venice; to the Botanical Gardens where the tree that inspired Tolkien's Tree-beard once stood. Between all this, the first meetings of the workshop at Eagle and Child, and agonizing over what to submit that very evening, Carson hasn't had time to consider Anders . . . or Anneliese.

The last thought makes him feel guilty, and it shows on his face when he says, "No—I think it'll go pretty late. But you guys have fun."

"You haven't been around very much."

He's surprised she's noticed. "I've been pretty busy."

Fidgeting with the sleeve of her oversized sweater, she says, "Can't you come?"

"Isn't Vivi going?" he hedges.

"Yeah—if Anders is somewhere, so is Vivi. So there won't be anyone, really."

"You know everyone."

She makes a face at his lackluster comment.

"I was hoping we could talk," she says finally. "I wanted to . . . "

"Is something wrong?"

"I guess a pub wouldn't be the best place anyway, but—"

"I'll try and be back in time," he says, and her

eyes snap to his. “We can’t go much past seven, and I think Blackwell’s will kick us out around then anyhow.”

She gives him a grateful smile, and it makes his heart beat fast. He wishes she could tell him, or least drop a heavier hint, about what she needs to talk to him about, but she’s fishing her keycard out of her wallet and telling him she’ll see him later. All he can do is trudge down the hallway in confusion.

He files it away under things to worry about later—a rather large file, already occupied by upcoming exams, the possibility of how bad his grades might be this semester, travelling logistics for winter break, and which classes to take next semester—when he sees the back of Mandy’s bouncy head of curls waiting for him in third quad.

She turns when she hears him coming down the steps and says, “Hi.”

He flushes from his toes all the way up to his cheeks. “Hey. How’re you?”

Her shoulders lift in an exaggerated shrug.

"Surviving," she says before leaning closer. "Just barely."

They're soon joined by the other three of their workshop: Alex, a lanky Scottish soccer player; Nora, a short girl with the roundest button nose Carson's ever seen; and Sundeep, another ASA student who's already had a book published back home. With their merry band all present, they head out of Jesus bound for Blackwell's. He enjoyed going to the Eagle and Child for their first workshops, but the pub ended up being a bit too loud in the end.

Instead, they've relocated to Carson's new favorite place in Oxford. It's a stiff competition, really, to be his favorite, but it's hard to beat one of the biggest bookstores he's ever seen. Floors and floors of books. He loves looking over the British editions of titles and the wide cabinets of notable Oxford authors. He loves the classics section and the fiction section and the biography section, and, when they hop up the stairs and come to it, the cozy café nestled in amongst the shelves.

After collecting steaming mugs of tea, they settle themselves on plush leather couches and chairs surrounding a low coffee table laden with magazines, book catalogs, and a few Dickens classics. Carson sits with Mandy in a loveseat as they all pull out manuscripts and laptops.

Mandy starts things off by making sure everyone has everyone else's contact information, confirms another meeting date, and then new manuscripts are passed around before they all decide to start on Alex's story.

Carson eases into the loveseat and the workshop, loving the talk of allegory, the discussion of dialogue, and the feel of Mandy's shoulder pressed against his. He tries not to blush when he thinks about it yet again, and out of the corner of his eye he watches her push a hunk of hair behind her ear for the fifth time.

When it's Carson's turn, he learns a lot of what

he already knows—the beginning plays the pronoun game, there should be a bit more dialogue between the middle and climax, it uses a nice amount of metaphor and description. He listens to it eagerly, willing it to give him the extra gumption he needs to finally write something new.

"While I read the bar scene I was definitely thinking of The King's Arms," Alex says with a smile, his finger on the scene in question in Carson's story.

"Hopefully that's a good thing," he says.

"It is—it's my favorite pub here, so well done."

Nora leans toward Alex, and with exasperated arched eyebrows says, "Does it really remind you of The King's Arms, or are you just hungry?"

"Aye," Alex says with a wink, not committing to either.

"Well then, let's do Nora and then go *eat*!" Mandy says.

When they've addressed all of Nora's concerns about use of second person narrative, they shuffle papers, close laptops, and reconvene down the street at The King's Arms. It's one of the pubs Carson hasn't gotten to yet—he maintains there should be some sort of pub Bingo card—but he immediately likes the oak bar and winged leather chairs.

Alex leads them to a booth and wastes no time ordering a round of pints, despite Nora's protest that beer is "quite disgusting." Looking mockingly offended, Alex says, "Nonsense," and heads to the bar.

Carson watches, amused, as Nora musses her hair and straightens the neckline of her sweater—pulling it a little lower—and wonders if Alex is ignorant or uninterested. Judging from his writing, he's the latter.

Feeling Mandy's fingers squeeze the inside of his elbow, he looks her way and sees her biting her lip, trying to keep back a smile. Instead they smile at each other, guiltily finding the situation funny. Sundeep sitting languidly engrossed in her menu, clueless, only widens their smiles.

An hour later, with a stomach heavy with ale and fish and chips, Carson leans back into the booth, happy to watch Sundeep thoroughly school Nora and Alex in a fierce game of darts.

"I think if those were knives rather than darts, she'd be quite an assassin," Carson says.

"She's definitely a woman of many talents," Mandy agrees, her head leaning ever so slightly on his shoulder. "Sometimes I think she's walked straight out of a book."

"That's probably why she's already published."

"Mm. I'm happy to pick her brain—she's wickedly good at dialogue."

He gives her a little nudge. "So're you."

Her fingers slip into his. "Flatterer."

Alex retreats to the booth as Sundeep shows Nora proper technique. Draining the last of his pint, he says, "Remind me never to piss her off."

"Well, if the newspaper says you died by dart, we'll know who it was, at least," Carson says.

Alex throws back his head and laughs. "Small favors."

When Nora seems satisfied she's learned the rudiments of dart-throwing, they pay the bar tab and head back to the college. Carson feels heady on the walk back, both from the pint and Mandy's hand wrapped around his, sheltered in his jacket pocket.

In third quad their party breaks up after confirming the next meeting. Mandy lingers, and Carson looks down at her, suddenly reluctant to leave too, searching his head for an excuse not to go back up to his room.

He blinks, and he thinks he's seeing things when her face comes closer to his. She gets up on her tiptoes, and he has just enough sense to lean down the rest of the way. She kisses him, and when he's recovered from the shock, he kisses her. She tastes warm, like ale and sugar, and for a long moment he forgets what his mouth is supposed to do against hers. He hasn't kissed anyone in a long time—not since a dumb high school party game of spin the bottle. He hasn't been interested in kissing anyone in a long time either—not since the day the FOR SALE sign went up in front of Anneliese's summer cabin, and they raced down to the beach where they stood with their toes in the icy water and she kissed him rather than saying goodbye.

He gratefully lets instinct take over, feeling the softness of her cheek and hair as he puts a tentative hand to her face. Her hands grip his jacket, and he can feel her pulse beating in her palms.

When she leans back too soon, he looks down at her, just making out the brightness of her eyes and curve of her smile in the dim overhead lights of the quad.

"Do you want to come up and watch a movie or something?" she asks breathlessly.

"Yeah," he says, equally breathless.

Taking his hand again, she leads him into one of the other dorm buildings, up to the fourth floor. Her room is neat—he expected nothing less—with what looks like an even mix of school and pleasure reading books standing in a line down the whole back length of her desk. He smiles at the collection of lumpy scarves hung on a collage of hooks on her wardrobe.

He agrees to the first thing she suggests as she scrolls through options on her computer, happy at whatever settles her the fastest into the chair next to him. With Mandy curled up beside him, her hand in his, and his mouth on hers more often than not, Carson doesn't think he's ever paid less attention to a movie.

Looking up from the piecemeal essay on the role of race in *Othello*, Carson gazes with bleary eyes out the window, startled to see that it's dark. For a moment he hopes it isn't that late—the sun disappears at four o'clock now that winter looms.

The clock on his computer tells him, however, that it is indeed past nine. Raking fingers through his hair, Carson leans back in the swivel chair and looks with abject disgust at his essay.

The sound of someone knocking at the front door takes a moment to register, but before he can push himself away from the desk, he hears Anders answer the door and chatter in the vestibule. For a moment he thinks he's hearing things, but no, there it is again, a soft knock. Pausing only long enough to flick on the lights of his room, Carson opens the door to find Anneliese standing there, Anders and Vivi close behind, oblivious to all else but each other.

"Hey," he says, smiling down at her. He fights the urge to rub his eyes.

"Hey. Anders says you didn't know if you're coming tonight."

He slumps a little against the doorframe, knowing that look in her eyes. He's seen it before, and it brings a wave of guilt rushing through him. She wanted to talk to him last weekend, and he, like an idiot, hadn't followed up, hadn't apologized for not making it then. The reason for why he wasn't there—Mandy's lips pressed against his, her fingers straying beneath the neck of his shirt—pops into his head.

"I've got an essay," he says, bland as oatmeal.

"Could you use a break?"

He sucks in a breath. He knows he should be disgusted at how easily his resolve melts, but she's looking at him, the corners of her eyes thrown into an uneasy shadow, and he has to know why.

Leaning around into the wardrobe, he pulls out a coat and grins. "Definitely."

He smiles as Anders whacks him on the shoulder. "There you are, mate," he says. "I was beginning to forget what you looked like."

"Probably not great," Carson says, suddenly wishing he had more than his fingers to comb through his hair.

"Essays do that to a man. That's why I avoid them at all costs," Anders says with a cavalier wink before he and Vivi saunter down the hall, the sequins on Vivi's skirt catching the florescent light.

"Those two are something," he says only loud enough for Anneliese to hear.

"They're either going to get married or have a very nasty breakup soon."

"Oh? Trouble in paradise?"

She shrugs as she walks through the door he holds for her. "Not really—that's just the kind they are, you know?"

"They get on really well."

"I haven't met anyone who didn't get on well with them."

He decides not to tell her how Mandy's nose involuntarily wrinkles every time she encounters Anders. Now *they* didn't get on well, from the beginning. Despite his laid-back charisma, Anders wasn't a fool, and he could easily tell when his charm was wasted on someone. And, as for Mandy . . . he suspects the charming villain in her latest story has a very real inspiration.

The usual group amasses in third quad before departing for, to Carson's immediate dislike, the Purple Turtle. He doesn't have anything against the nightclub personally, but he'd hoped this would be a more pub-oriented outing, something where he could conceivably hear his own thoughts and carry on a conversation with Anneliese.

"I'm sorry we didn't talk," he says as they head up Ship Street, wanting to make sure he says it before reaching the club. "I got sidetracked." The story of his life these days.

"It's alright," she says, but he can't help feeling it isn't. "It probably wasn't important."

He doesn't question further as Nathan falls into step at Anneliese's other side. He feels a spark of dislike toward the classicist, who, since being accepted into the group by the others has been indifferent toward Carson. He wallows in silence, halfheartedly listening to their conversation about '90s rock music. She's bubbly with Nathan, and Carson can't help the jealousy that rises in his chest whenever she throws a smile Nathan's way. Carson gets barely more than a few quiet sentences while Nathan, as if *he's* the one who's known her since childhood, gets smiles and laughs and a constant stream of words.

His mood doesn't improve as they turn down a narrow alley, descending stairs into the subterranean bar; nor does it when they select a semicircular booth which he slumps into gratefully; not even as he nurses a pint Anders procures for him before claiming a section of dancefloor with Vivi. It definitely doesn't improve when, after a few minutes' hesitation, Anneliese disappears into the crowd with Nathan. He catches passing glimpses of her, her long blonde hair undone and swaying against her back, and the sight of Nathan's hands on her only makes him sulk.

To distract himself from the sight and the confusing mix of jealousy and guilt, he turns toward Niall and Jordan and joins their poker game, having borrowed a deck and chips from the games corner. From the first hand he's dealt, he knows it isn't in the cards for him tonight. The sticky darkness of the club feels claustrophobic somehow, the air too hot, the music too loud, the lights too neon. Despite losing two hands in a row, he continues to play, refusing to look at the dance floor. Why did she want him to come so badly if she was just going to be with Nathan the whole time? He feels the beginnings of a headache flitting behind his right eye.

He's down twenty pounds and two pints before he feels someone slip into the booth beside him.

Anneliese smiles languidly at him, smelling like honey and sweat and vodka. "Sorry," she says. "What're you playing?" She leans her head against him, taking a peek at his hand. Patting his forearm, she says, "That's no good."

Quite agreeing, Carson folds, easing back so that his head can rest against the booth. He feels her tug at his arm.

"Didn't you want to dance?"

"Not even a little bit," he says. The blissful haze retreats from her eyes, and he amends quickly, "I'm doing everyone a favor by not."

She's smiling again. "Such a spoilsport."

"Sorry," he says, leaning toward her so he doesn't have to shout. "I don't mean to be a buzzkill."

"I'm happy you came. I feel better when you come."

He's about to ask her why when Nathan rejoins them, two drinks in hand. He sets them in front of Anneliese and pushes in beside her, forcing Carson to shift further into the booth to make room.

He watches Anneliese carefully as she says something to Nathan. Nathan presses one of the cocktails into her hands, and she sips at it, finally giving him a nod of approval. She turns to offer Carson a sip, but he loses the name of it over the noise. He declines, though it doesn't seem to matter as Nathan's hand slips around her to rest on her hip.

She faces him, but Carson can't hear words, only muffled tone. He stiffens when Nathan's mouth descends to hers, his hands on her shoulder and the small of her back. Resisting the urge to slam his head onto the table, Carson muses darkly that there *are* worse things than writing essays.

He's trying to retreat into a storyline, desperately wafting through some snippets of plot he likes to ruminate on before falling asleep, when Anneliese's elbow jams into him. His eyes snap to her.

Nathan's hands are everywhere, his mouth trying to move down from her mouth to her neck. Anneliese pushes him, saying something sharp. She gets a palm against his face and shoves it, squirming into the booth, away from him.

Without thinking, Carson puts an arm around her and pulls her toward him. She kicks at Nathan as she goes, her eyes throwing daggers. Nathan jumps up, shouting something that's lost in the noise of the club, and storms away.

"You okay?"

Her breath is coming in rapid bursts and a line of perspiration wets her brow. She jams a hunk of hair behind her ear and glares in the direction Nathan's disappeared.

"You wanna leave?"

At this she nods ferociously, and Carson doesn't need to be told twice. Retreating from the club, Carson helps Anneliese up the stairs into the alley. Their breaths come in hot clouds as they turn back onto Cornmarket.

When Anneliese stumbles, he catches her the best he can then rips off his coat and puts it around her. He immediately misses having a refuge for his hands. The silent, if slightly zigzagging walk back toward Jesus is unbearable.

"Did he hurt you?" he forces himself to ask.

She takes a moment to answer, having to concentrate on her footfalls. The cold night air seems to have sobered her a little, because she looks back at him with rapidly clearing eyes. "No. Just felt like being a jerk, apparently."

"Has he done that before?"

"Not as bad."

He can't help an exasperated sigh. "Then why do you talk to him? Why do you smile so much at him?" Immediately he wishes he could reach out a hand, grab his words, and shove them right back into his mouth.

Nibbling on a thumbnail, she says finally, "Smiling distracts people." Before he can comment or question, she turns to him and says, "Thank you."

"For what?"

"For coming. For walking me back."

"You're doing a pretty good job on your own," he observes as he tugs his keycard from his wallet to open the side door into the college.

"I've had practice. Though it'd be a different story if I'd listened to Vivi and worn heels."

On their way through third quad, they cross paths with Mandy, hopping up the steps from fourth quad with the rest of the workshop group in tow. She smiles when she sees him. Too late does he realize that maybe he should be apprehensive about Mandy and Anneliese meeting, that maybe he should've tried to avoid it altogether, but Mandy's already making her way over.

She greets the two of them, her eyes lingering only a moment on Carson's jacket hanging on Anneliese's shoulders. He can't help feeling her eyes, a little too sharp, are purposefully staying on him rather than taking in Anneliese. Alex, Nora, and Sundeep are close behind. Carson shakes Alex's hand and smiles at the girls, the sudden thought hitting him that he'd much rather have been with them tonight.

He quickly introduces them all to Anneliese, willing himself not to flush red.

"We're in Economics together," Mandy says with a smile of recognition toward Anneliese.

Anneliese nods, returning the smile, but Carson sees how stiff she is. This probably isn't the time.

"Are you done with the essay?" Carson asks, drawing Mandy's attention to him.

She puts her hands to her cheeks and pulls them down, making an over-exaggerated face. "It's murder."

Alex and Sundeep make similar, unenthusiastic noises about the essay. "*Othello*'s got to be my least favorite Shakespeare play," Nora supplies.

Carson grins conspiratorially. "I think it's getting the better of me."

"Most definitely."

He feels Anneliese shifting beside him and says to Mandy, "I'll text you later?"

She smiles and agrees. Saying farewell to the others, Carson and Anneliese hop up the stairs to their dorm building.

Anneliese doesn't say anything until they're standing in front of their respective doors.

"Could I come in for a while?" she asks.

"Sure."

He lunges as deftly as he can after entering his room for the food wrappers littering his desk. While tidying up the signs of overworked studenthood, out of the corner of his eye, Carson sees Anneliese sit in one of the chairs beneath the bay window. After making two mugs of chamomile tea and munching on the day's ration of plastic-wrapped cookies, Carson slumps into the other chair.

"I'm sorry for dragging you along," Anneliese finally says. "We didn't really hang out, did we?"

"It's alright."

"I thought you'd want to dance."

He tries his best to grin. "Again, doing the world a favor by not."

After folding her legs beneath her, Anneliese absentmindedly swirls her cookie through the tea.

"Anneliese, what was it you wanted to talk to me about? Is something wrong?"

She doesn't immediately answer. "I just wanted to talk."

"About what?"

"I hadn't seen you in a while," she hedges.

"Are you alright?"

"Yeah. Are you?"

"Yeah."

Her phone begins to ring, but rather than answering it, she glares inscrutably into her tea, ignoring the tone until a little beep informs them someone's left a voicemail.

"Do you need to—?"

She's shaking her head. "I don't wanna talk to her." She sighs. "She'd freak if she saw this." She indicates the hip-hugging blue dress she has on. Carson suspects it's Vivi's—meaning it hits Anneliese's knee where on Vivi it'd rise to the upper thigh.

"Yeah?"

"Oh yeah."

The phone rings again, and it's met with the same pinched face.

After two rings, Carson says, "Are you sure you shouldn't answer? Something might be wrong." In his family, two calls so close together meant someone was in the hospital.

Anneliese frowns, a large tear running down her face. She wipes it away quickly, shaking her head. "I don't want to talk to her," she repeats.

"Why?" he asks, barely more than a whisper.

"She's not exactly pleasant." Anneliese wipes at her eye again. "You know my mom."

Carson didn't know Mrs. Johansson at all, but from what he'd seen of her, he inferred a great deal. And so had his mother.

"She hates me for coming here, which is exactly why I did."

Carson doesn't know what to do or say, so he sits there quietly, watching her. The words are tumbling out of her, some slurred together, as if the alcohol is still having an effect.

"You know, she's threatening not to pay my way back for break because I want to spend half of it with my dad. She'd rather leave me stranded here, alone." Her chest convulses in a sob as the mug wobbles in her hand. "She's moved us around seven times for her job, just picking up and leaving without notice. I came home from school once with everything packed up in boxes again. She'd just left a note, 'We're going to Seattle. Went to get more boxes.' That's how she told me."

He listens as she tells him about finally settling in L.A., putting down roots though she didn't overly like southern California. How her mother had discouraged her making friends, her reaching out to her father. How when she'd learned Anneliese got into Oxford, she hadn't even congratulated her, just said, "Oh."

She confesses to slipping grades as well, but whereas Carson's prospective bad marks mean a less than auspicious start to college, hers could very well mean her mother pulling the plug on Oxford. Anneliese did her best to secure scholarships, but in the end, her mother had to make up the difference.

Anneliese talks late into the night, but Carson can't decide what to do, doesn't know if he should touch her or speak. Covering his mouth with his hand, his mind races with her summer smiles, her search for adventure, her desire to always be outdoors, out of her house. His heart sinks down to about his feet, and he finally reaches out, putting a gentle hand on her shoulder. But all he can do is sit there, again helplessly listening as she cries.

Carson shoves his hands into his pockets, his fingers fiddling with his wallet as he waits for Mandy. He passes the time by trying to come up with a way he can help Anneliese. His thoughts turn sour when he sees Nathan striding across third quad. They lock eyes for a moment, and then Nathan presses on with a scowl. Carson has happily cut ties with Nathan, moving across Classics class to sit as far away from him as possible. They both know why.

Mandy slips her hand into his arm, and he blinks, suddenly drawn back into the present. A slow smile spreads over his face.

"You look faraway."

He shakes his head. "Lost in thought."

"So is the cross we writers must bear."

Heading out to the Eagle and Child, Carson likes the feel of her warm, smaller hand in his. He likes the square tips of her fingers, the two freckles dotting her left knuckles.

"Did you finish the chapter like you wanted?" he asks.

"Yes, finally! It was fighting me, but I think I finally hammered out the conflict."

"Yeah? Is the cop going to leave the waitress like you—?"

"She's an artist now."

"Ah, sorry," he says with a smile. Mandy never can settle on a career for her heroines. "Did he leave her then?"

"Yes, which is probably why it was so hard to write. John is a right bastard sometimes."

He likes how she talks about her characters like they're living, breathing people, how her eyes light up when she divulges the twists and turns of their lives. Sinking into her fantasy is a welcome relief, because he feels too troubled to find his own.

"Will they get back together?"

She lifts her shoulders in a light shrug, grinning up at him impishly. "I haven't decided yet. But truth be told, I'm a romantic at heart."

"Why did he break it off?"

Her eyes shine. "Ah, that. Well, he found out that she's harboring the very fugitive he's been hunting." She grips his arm and says as confidentially as she would a real secret, "But it's really her brother."

"Dun dun duuun."

She smiles at the dramatic theme music, but by the time they've ordered and claimed a table, she's frowning that frown that tells him they're about to discuss a plot point.

"But do you think it's too cliché?" she asks.

"That probably depends on what their relationship is—the brother and sister, I mean."

"What do you mean?"

"Well, we've seen a loving sibling cover up for another, and we've also seen the other end of the spectrum—a sibling forced to do it. Something in the middle, though, could be really interesting."

"Like she loves him, but their relationship is all but sturdy."

"Right. The crime he's supposed to go away for could definitely rock the boat."

She rests her chin in her palm. "Murder most foul."

"I'd say that's a fair-sized wedge between them, then."

She nods, considering, but Carson's distracted by the muffled sound of his text alert. Resisting the conditioning to dive into his coat pocket and answer, he keeps his focus on Mandy. It's her turn to look faraway, and he watches her with an inward smile. He wonders if he looks something like that when story-building: mouth to one side, cheek dimpled, slight frown, dreamy eyes.

His phone suddenly belts a melody of alerts,

almost keeping an even rhythm as a flurry of texts come to his phone. It's so many that he can see the thoughts retreating from Mandy's eyes as they flick toward him.

"Should you . . .?"

He nods, finally withdrawing the phone. Frowning, he hurriedly reads over the ten new messages from Anneliese. He takes a sharp breath as he opens his phone so he can look at them in order.

"Is everything alright?"

He shakes his head vaguely.

The texts start relatively normal, asking if he's in, but get increasingly worrisome, the spelling slipping, the thoughts becoming incoherent. But the last one sticks with him, fills his eyes and brain. Can you come, please?

"Carson?"

Mandy's voice finally registers, and he looks up at her, indecision rearing its ugly, waffling head. He doesn't want to run out on Mandy—more than that, he doesn't want to leave her. He wants to be with her, to talk about novels and writing and the newest *Star Wars* movie and her dad's latest adventure in remodeling and why fantasy is better than sci-fi.

But last week, Anneliese needed someone to trust and she chose him. She's asking for him now. Their years apart don't matter right now; whatever her reason for not contacting him, they're still friends.

"I have to run back," he says, beginning to stand. "I have a friend—she's having some problems and I need to see that she's okay. I'll be right back?"

Mandy nods slowly, keeping her face carefully impassive. "Alright." She tries smiling. "But if you're gone too long, your chips are fair game."

He covers her hand on the table with his and squeezes. "Thanks."

Carson doesn't know what he expects to find when he gets back, but along the way he tries not to think about it. The walk back to the college takes an agonizingly long time, even though just a while ago it had taken him and Mandy no time at all.

When he finally rasps his knuckles against Anneliese's front door, he's preparing himself for the unknown.

Vivi answers. "Oh thank god," she says, her mouth a displeased line. She gestures at Anneliese's door, behind her to the right. "She's been going on all afternoon."

Carson mumbles a thank you as she lets him cross into the anteroom, though he doesn't think she deserves one for her apathetic summary of the situation. Vivi watches expectantly as he knocks on Anneliese's door. They wait for an answer, but when none comes, he tests the handle. Glancing at Vivi over his shoulder, he opens it quietly.

The room is dark, smelling of tea and laundry detergent. A little light seeps in through the window, illuminating an empty chair and desk. A lump on the bed shifts, and he sees Anneliese's golden head just above the covers.

He crosses to her, telling himself not to shove his hands into his pockets. He's dealt with tantrums before—as the oldest of four, he's seen his fair share. But this isn't a tantrum and Anneliese isn't his tempestuous youngest sister, Ellie. Trying to ignore the blaring fact that he hasn't a clue what to do, he awkwardly sits on the edge of her bed, putting as little of his body on it as he can manage without falling off. She sits up, her knees tucked beneath her blankets.

"You came," she says into the dark.

"You asked me to."

Her silhouette nods, and he can just make out her shoulders beginning to shake. He steels himself for her tears, but they still catch him off guard nonetheless. When she reaches out a hand, he takes it, nearly crushing her trembling fingers in his own.

"Did something happen?" he asks softly when her sobs subside.

Anneliese wipes at her face with her free palm. Even in the dark he can see the deep frown lining her brow.

"I had to meet with my Econ professor today. I'm going to fail."

"But what about the final? Can't you—?"

"If I ace it I might fail a little less. I'll be put on academic probation—and I'll have to retake it next semester."

"That's not so bad," he lies. "You'll do fine the next time around."

She shakes her head as if it weighs three times what it should. Finally she lets it sink to her knees. "She won't let me come back. I'll never—" Her head flies up. "I don't want to go home! I don't want to see her!"

He holds her hand tighter. "You don't want to be here over break by yourself, though."

"It'd be better than being with her."

Carson sucks in a breath as her head slumps back down. Silence creeps between them while he sits, thinking.

"Hey," he says, "what if you came back with me?"

For a long moment she doesn't say anything. She raises her head. "What?"

"I know my family wouldn't mind—they'd love

to see you. It'd be nice to go back to the U.S., at least, right?"

"Carson . . . "

"Just think about it, alright? You should do whatever you think is best, but the offer stands, if you want it."

"Okay." She wraps her other hand around his. "Thank you."

Nodding, Carson tries to smile, though he knows she can't see it. "It'll be fun."

After a moment, she says, "Carson?"

"Yeah?"

"Would you stay for a while?"

He swallows. "Yeah, sure."

While Anneliese eases back under her billowing comforter, Carson texts Mandy with his one free hand, explaining as best he can and apologizing profusely.

She texts back almost immediately, and he turns the ringer off so it won't bug Anneliese.

Is your friend OK?

I think so. I think she'll be better tomorrow, but she probably shouldn't be alone.

I see.

I'm really sorry. I swear I'll make it up to you.

I should think so :)

Suspecting Mandy doesn't mean the smiley face, he sighs. But the axe is dropped. Carson scoots back into the bed a little farther so that he can lean his head against the wall.

They don't talk very much after that, but Anneliese keeps his hand, their one large fist, resting on her hip. Her grip doesn't slacken even as she drifts to sleep, and he's relieved to finally listen to her soft breaths instead of her sobs.

Carson didn't know he could ever sympathize so much with the little Dutch boy with his finger in the dyke. He's never been one to cram, always organized, always having flash cards and flow charts at the ready, but after his first two final exams with two more looming ahead, he feels like he's putting Band-Aids on something that needs stitches.

The Philosophy final had gone about as badly as expected, and he knows from now until the end of time he'll hate anyone who says they're a Philosophy major. World History went a bit better, which he wholeheartedly attributed to the blue hyperlinks of Wikipedia. Now only Classics and English stood between him and his flight to San Francisco, but when he should have felt confident, maybe even a little cocky, at the prospect, all he feels is dread. He should know these subjects, had been reading about these authors all his life. But after the first few weeks of slacking off reading, he's become Sisyphus, rolling his rock up the mountain but never able to reach the summit. *There*, he thinks with chagrin, *I did learn something*.

He happily gives in to a minute's reprieve to answer the knock at the front door.

"Hi," Anneliese says, her arms clutching her book bag to her chest. "Can I study in here? Vivi and Anders are having a shouting match."

"You called it," he says darkly, opening the door wider.

She looks about as tired as he feels, and they silently retreat into his room. Setting her things about one of the green chairs, Anneliese pulls her feet up under her.

"I'd offer you tea, but I've used up my stores.

I'm on a strict diet of caffeine and shortbread cookies."

"I brought mine," she says with a tired smile, making the creases under her eyes run long.

She makes up the mugs as Carson fills the heater with water from the bathroom sink. A few minutes later they're sitting facing each other, sipping hot Earl Grey, waiting for the tea to make some small difference.

He makes a banal remark about how amazing it is that they've been converted to tea in only a few months, and she replies equally mildly that when the coffee is so poor, one makes do.

A text alert draws his numbed attention, and Carson gazes down dismally at Mandy asking him if he wants to study together. If anyone could help him keep the Austen heroines straight and explain why each of their storylines mattered to the social structure of early-nineteenth century England, it's Mandy. But to teach him, he'd have to admit how little he knows, how thoroughly the semester has defeated him, and his pride isn't shrunk enough to let her see it. He pushes the phone to the far side of the desk without replying.

When he's read through the same line of Plato seven times, he admits defeat and switches to an academic journal article discussing the Brontë sisters. He has a bit of an easier time with it—even though he at best skimmed *Jane Eyre*—and is halfway finished when Anneliese's phone begins to ring.

The strangled sigh that escapes her lips draws his gaze. With a pursed mouth she answers, and Carson doesn't need three guesses to determine who it is.

"Mm-hmm . . . Yeah, I know . . . No . . . No, I don't . . . Mom, I . . . Because I don't. You can't just . . . That isn't fair, I . . . Fine, if that's how you feel . . . Fine. Bye."

Carson waits on pins and needles for her to say something, though he stares determinedly at the article, unable to read it but not wanting to intrude. From the corner of his eye he sees her looking out the bay windows with a glassy stare, the last light of the day framing her in a gray halo.

"I can't go home with you." Her voice is so soft that he strains to hear each word.

He tries to keep the uneasiness from his face. "No?"

She shakes her head, still looking out the window, her chin propped in her palm. "No. She says if I won't come home, she won't pay for the flight. She doesn't want me to stay with your family or see my dad. So I'm stuck here after all."

"You couldn't go with Vivi? I'm sure she wouldn't mind."

"They're going to Monaco for the holidays."

"Oh."

She wipes at her face and tries to grin. "It's alright. I've never been that into Christmas."

"Still," he says. He picks at a thumbnail. "What if . . . I paid for half your ticket, could you cover the rest?"

Her gaze slowly swings to him, the words seeming to take a moment to wash over her. "Carson . . . "

"If you want to come home, then you should come home. I can cover half." At least, he thinks he can. He tries not to check his bank account all that often. But if memory serves, with a little scrimping and saving on meals for a while afterward and dipping into his savings, he could do it.

"I can't ask you to do that."

He shrugs. "You aren't. I'm offering."

"You'd seriously do that?"

"Yeah. My flight's in two days. Late. We can call the airline tomorrow and see if they have any leftover seats and then try booking it with two cards. I'm sure they've seen worse."

She's nodding along, though her gaze has dropped and won't rise to meet his. "Thank you," she says in a small voice.

"So you'll come?"

"Yes."

He smiles. "Good."

With a force that keeps him pinned in his seat and steals the breath out of his lungs, her eyes meet his. "Carson, you're a good friend. While I . . . haven't been."

His fingertips are tingling. Air comes rushing back into his chest, but all he can get out is, "I'm sure you had a reason."

Her mouth arches up as if she'll laugh, but nothing comes out. "I wish I did. Everything happened so fast, the divorce, the move. Mom moved us to San Jose and I just sort of . . . I didn't really think about anything from back when they were married. It only reminded me of how much I hated her for breaking everything up. But that isn't an excuse—you didn't ruin everything like her. If anything you . . . you were my only real friend. And I just left."

His shoulders lift with effort in a heavy shrug, making his chest feel hollow inside. "We were friends. We *are* friends. I'm not mad, Anneliese."

It isn't quite a lie—he's not sure *mad* describes how he feels—but it still pains him to say it.

"Not even if I deserve it?"

"Not even if you deserve it. And you don't. It wasn't your fault."

"I still could have—"

"It's alright," he says it. Because it is. Maybe it doesn't feel alright now, not fresh, but deep down he somewhat suspected it was her reason. The house in Tahoe was a reminder of when she'd been happy, and remembering it only underscored how unhappy she is now.

Wiping her eyes one more time, Anneliese arranges her face into a smile. "Thank you." She rises from her chair so she can put her arms around his neck. "Thank you."

When she goes to draw away, she pauses, her arms still about him. Her eyes flick down to his mouth, and when his drift down to hers, she leans in again, pressing their lips together. He wants to imagine she tastes like summer, like crisp alpine air and icy snowmelt water, but she doesn't.

As she presses into him harder, nearly in his lap, he says in a ragged breath, "Anneliese . . . "

Her forehead on his, she shakes her head once. "Just kiss me, okay?"

"Okay."

So he does. He pulls her into him, her thighs on either side of his hips, and he lets himself, for a moment, believe she tastes, and feels, the same. He kisses her like he should have that first time, as if it can undo what's been done, as if he can keep her close now.

But that's the last he thinks. He lets his mind go blank, lets his body take over. He feels, smells, hears, but doesn't think. Everywhere she's soft. His fingers touch the warm skin of her stomach and lower back. He pushes up her plush sweater, and she tugs off his slick cotton shirt. Buttons make little *pops*, zippers come undone with crisp *clicks*. He doesn't think about how he fumbles, just feels frustration then relief when she takes over and seems to know what to do. The only thing he tries not to hear as they fall into bed is the distant sound of a text alert, one— the back of his muddled brain realizes—he should feel guilty about.

The first thought that crosses Carson's mind the next morning is that it's too bright for his alarm not to have gone off. His eyes fly open to behold the traitorous red numbers gleaming in the soft morning light: 7:54. His exam's at eight.

Something shifts beside him, and with reverent dread Carson slowly looks over at Anneliese, still lying beside him. Her golden hair is mussed, the little baby hairs around her face like duckling down. She looks for all the world like she's at peace. Carson envies her.

Last night comes crashing down on him with its

full weight, and he lies there, pinned to the bed. He glances down at her with a strangled look.

He needs to get away. 7:55. Attempting to find a happy medium between rushing out of the room and being carefully quiet not to wake Anneliese, Carson zips his pants with a grimace, fetches a clean shirt and jacket from the wardrobe, and leaves with two pens and his keycard in his pocket.

He flies to his English exam and arrives to an already packed room. Pointedly avoiding the curly brown head that bobs his way when he enters, he nods sheepishly at the professor's arched eyebrows at his being one minute late and interrupting directions.

When it's put in front of him, Carson looks down at the exam form as he would the hangman's noose. He sees the letters forming words, but momentarily forgets how to read. The shuffling of papers rouses him, and he furtively looks about, watching his classmates take out and organize sheaves of notes. If it's possible, his heart sinks further down, below the floor, into the Earth's mantle. He could've brought a page of notes. What he was doing instead of copying out a cheat sheet makes his face burn.

Now he's left to the mercy of vocab words, terms, excerpt passages, overarching themes, and his own overwhelmed brain. He tries calming himself, putting his pen to the paper on the first essay question, but nothing comes. Forcing himself, he watches a messy version of his usual scrawl come flowing from the pen tip.

As he's turning the first page over, he glances at the clock only to have his heart jump miles back up into his throat. Not letting himself merely stare blankly at the questions, he reads, searches his memory.

The sound of the first people turning in their exams makes his pulse thrum harder in his ears. He's aware of Mandy's gaze momentarily on him as she collects her things from her desk after turning in the exam.

His shoulders sag in abject defeat when the professor calls that the time's up. He can't even take heart that he isn't the only one using up precious extra seconds to finish his last sentences. He knows, beyond a doubt, that their exams are infinitely better than his. Refusing to meet the professor's eye as he adds his sorry contribution to the pile of exams, Carson retreats from the room.

For a moment he contents himself that it's over—it's out of his hands, and now he'll have a few days to think of how to explain everything to his mother. He's forming an attack plan for his Classics exam tomorrow morning, when he spots Mandy sitting on a bench below one of the window casements of the dining hall, her ankles crossed and her hands in her lap. Sundeep stands close, talking to her.

Mandy's face turns toward him, and he knows he can't keep walking back to the dorms. He should explain it to her, should put to words why he's been so cagey. He sees different emotions flick across her eyes as she watches him approach. Sundeep lifts her head to see him coming. Her mouth becomes a grim line, and she barely nods at him before turning on her heels and heading into the dining hall.

"Hi," Mandy says, her grin pained.

"Hi."

"Can we talk a minute? Or do you need to run somewhere?" It isn't a jab; he knows she means nothing by it, but his guilt makes sure it's a hammer-stroke to his heart.

He sits down on the bench, not close enough to touch.

He hears her draw in a breath. "Are you alright?"

Swallowing, he nods. "Yeah. I've had kinder tests, though."

"That's not what I'm talking about."

"I know."

Her gaze drops to her lap where her thumb is picking off the glossy red nail polish from her opposite index finger. "You look tired."

"Yeah," he says on a sigh.

"I haven't heard from you. Nobody has."

"I've been . . . " Plowing a hand through his hair, he feels his courage deflate. Why can't he spit it out? Mandy deserves the truth. He's made a mess of things.

"Carson." She scoots a little closer on the bench so that he's forced to look at her. "It's alright if you don't want to tell me. I wish you would, but . . . Maybe it's best if you don't, really." Her eyes, growing glassy, drop again.

All he can do is make a meek comment about a friend needing him.

"And there's nothing wrong with that. You need to do what you think is best. I don't want to be an added stress."

He winces for the hundredth time that morning. "Mandy, believe me, you aren't."

He can see the comment doesn't sit well, that it brings up more questions, but for a long while she's silent.

"Then it's something else, then?" She shakes her head. "It doesn't matter. Look, Carson, what I'm trying to say is this: It's alright if you don't want a relationship, I just wish you could've told me. The fact is, I rather do want a relationship. With you. But it seems I guessed wrong about what you wanted. So I think it's best if we leave it there, don't you?"

Her words make his guilt, devastation, and anger at himself coalesce into a hard knot in the center of his chest. He didn't know he could ever feel so bad, so low.

"If that's what you want," is all he can think to say.

She closes her eyes for a long moment, her face contorted, and he realizes she's holding in a sob. His heart thumps painfully in his chest, but before he can do anything she fixes him with a teary stare and says, "It's not."

Then she's gone, through to the dining hall, leaving Carson in an empty second quadrangle. Resting his elbows on his knees, he presses his nose into his steepled fingers.

A soft breeze rustles the ivy hanging behind him, and the quiet noise makes him wish he were heading back to an empty room. He might, actually. But he knows if he does, it'll feel worse. Which is a good thing. He should feel worse.

So he sits there, unmoving, as the college wakes up around him. A sore spot in his chest throbs, and just to torture himself, he acknowledges what it means. He wants to go home.

Why he thought it'd be a good idea to take a final and a transatlantic flight all in the same day is beyond Carson. Handing the British Airlines employee his boarding pass, all he feels while following the other passengers down the movable gangway is a sort of muffled relief. Not excitement, not annoyance, not longing. He just wants to sleep.

Slumping down into his aisle seat, his eyes glaze. His Classics exam had gone about as well as he thought it would—meaning that while he couldn't always separate Socrates from Aristotle from Plato, he was nevertheless expected to.

Movement against the grain of the slow march

toward the tail of the plane draws his attention. A woman with a broad-brimmed hat that looks better suited for the Kentucky Derby than an eleven-hour battle with the jet stream is plodding her way toward another woman who waits by a seat across the aisle from Carson. Anneliese waits behind her as the two women speak quickly about their seats and Anneliese's, switching with her so they can sit together. Anneliese quietly stares at that ridiculous hat until it's all settled and done. Finally, the woman with the hat gives Anneliese a firm hug, which she takes stiffly, and heads off with the other woman. The regular flow of boarders resumes, and more than one person looks relieved as the women disappear in the direction of their seats.

After sitting down and stowing her backpack beneath the seat in front of her, Anneliese catches Carson's gaze. She dons a forced grin and he returns it, relieved when a rumpled businessman blocks his view.

If Carson thought his talk with Mandy had been

painful, returning to find Anneliese dressed and just about to leave was a new level of torture. There was no shouting, just a silent sort of awkwardness that passed between them, that this wasn't how it should be. While they'd been nothing but polite to each other when securing her last-minute ticket and even during the last two hours of small talk in Heathrow, it still feels as if something has been ruined.

Soon after the plane takes off, Anneliese curls her legs up under her and all but disappears under the airplane blanket, only resurfacing when dinner is served two hours later. Carson tries not to watch her from the corner of his eye as he pokes at his portion of what the flight attendant assures him is chicken.

Even though a *Lord of the Rings* marathon on the personal screen set into the seat in front of his takes up the better part of the flight, he finds his attention (sparse as it already is) straying to Anneliese's softly sleeping form. He wants to find the right thing to say, to make this all go away.

Something tugs on his chest as he watches them

descend toward the Bay out the window. There's fog—of course—but landing doesn't take too long, nor does taxiing. Getting off the plane and through customs is another story.

Trying not to glare at the international tourists gliding through customs while he—a full-blooded citizen who'd been born only thirty miles away—and other returning citizens wait in the longer, slower line, Carson contemplates just lying on the ground and admitting defeat.

"It looks like we brought the English weather with us," Carson says as he checks his phone's inauspicious weather app.

"Probably."

"Are you happy it's over? Exams, I mean."

"Definitely."

Carson bites the inside of his cheek to keep from uttering any more painfully stupid small talk. He's never been happier to see a customs agent and steps forward with his passport and declaration form.

Once they've gotten through customs and

collected Anneliese's checked suitcase, it's only a few minutes before Carson's being enfolded in his father's impressive wingspan. He inhales sharply, taking in the woodsy smell of his father, and a wave of emotion threatens to make him start bawling right there in the middle of SFO. He chalks it up to the lack of sleep, but when his father makes to let him go, he presses his face into his shoulder and lingers a moment longer.

With a whack on the shoulder, his father smiles down at him. "How the hell are you?"

"Beat," Carson says. No one-word summary had ever been truer.

"I believe it. I had jet lag for days coming back from settling you in." His eyes flick over Carson's shoulder to where Anneliese stands behind him, having been looking away to give them privacy. He smiles and steps to her, embracing her almost as hard as he had Carson. "It's good to see you, Anneliese."

Anneliese cracks a smile, and Carson's relieved

to find it genuine. "Thank you for having me for Christmas."

"Don't mention it. The more mouths to eat my wife's Christmas ham, the better. Means less of it will end up in god-awful casseroles later." Winking mischievously, he takes Anneliese's suitcase from her and leads them toward short-term parking, his flannel-encased shoulders maneuvering the crowd easily.

"We really are happy to have you here," Carson says to her.

"And I'm happy to be here." She touches his arm. "Really."

He wants to feel reassured, but, as his father guides the SUV out of the labyrinthine parking garage, he doesn't. With Anneliese in the back seat, Carson has the crushing realization that she'll be there all break—a reminder. Propping his elbow on the door, his head sinks into his hand.

He doesn't really see the ride home. Doesn't notice the city around him, not the hilly pass through the coastal range dotted with wind turbines into the Central Valley, not the capital. He barely registers how the land eventually begins to rise again, the valley giving way to foothills. He's always felt at home in the hills, taking comfort in elevation and winding roads, but even the sight of the road steepening, braced on either side by pine trees, can't bolster his mood.

Snow-dusted trees welcome them to Tahoe. The lake itself is startlingly blue, surrounded by the white and gray of the snowy Sierras. The steeply peaked roofs are covered in soft white blankets, and the swirling clouds overhead, his father says, promise a few flurries during the night. Carson watches with mixed feelings as they turn onto their street. He thinks maybe he'll have forgotten a bend in the road, a tree, a boulder, the angle of his house's roof, the color of the front porch. But it's all the same, he remembers it exactly, and it both heartens and saddens him.

They're barely out of the SUV—his father's still

coaxing Anneliese's suitcase from the back—when they're set upon. A high screech comes from the front door as feet pound the porch steps. The force of Ellie and Jake's impact nearly knocks him over, and he stumbles back a step. Ellie wraps all of her limbs around his leg as Jake squeezes the life out of him, his ten-year-old arms surprisingly tight around his waist. He can barely get a breath in before his sixteen-year-old sister Amy comes out too.

"Carson, Carson! Look!" Ellie smiles up with two missing front teeth.

"Just like a hockey player," he teases, making Ellie scowl.

"We had to hold her down. I pulled them out," Jake boasts.

"And how much did you get?"

"*Five* dollars," Ellie says gleefully, producing the rumpled bill to lord over Jake.

Finally Ellie unwraps from his leg, letting him get a better balance. She smiles up at him, and he realizes with a pang in his chest that she's nearly as tall as Jake now. He puts a hand on her head, tears threatening to come to the surface again.

"Alright, everybody back," his mother commands from the porch. "I want to get a look at my firstborn."

His siblings back up, letting her through, though Ellie keeps hold of his left hand with the wickedly defiant smile only the youngest can get away with.

His mother smiles at him, putting her hands on either side of his face. "Hi, baby."

Hot moisture pricks at his eyes. "Hi, Mom."

Drawing herself up onto her toes so she can wrap fierce arms around his neck, she says, "It's good to have you home."

"Carson, we're going down to the lake. Come with us."

Slowly turning from his computer, Carson regards Jake and his friend Mark with a mix of apathy and mild annoyance. He shakes his head, saying, "Can't right now."

Jake rolls his eyes, his shoulders slumping in exaggeratedly bad posture. He sums up: "You never do anything with us."

"I've only been back three days."

"Could've fooled me," Jake says, his gaze now poignant and purposeful. "Your room isn't that great anyway. It doesn't even have the TV in it anymore."

"I noticed, thanks."

Jake sticks out his tongue as he follows Mark down the hall. Carson hears the backdoor swing open and their feet as they stomp down onto the path that leads to the icy shoreline.

His brother couldn't understand that he's hiding out, only really trying to avoid one person. Coming out of his room means facing Anneliese. He's successfully dodged all of his mother's suggestions of taking Anneliese to some of their old favorite haunts, instead letting Amy flaunt her new driver's license and take her. For her part, Anneliese doesn't seem to mind—at least, Carson couldn't read anything past her mild smile and acquiescing politeness. Which, Carson knows, is actually a bad thing.

Running an agitated hand through his hair, Carson looks back at the webpage, hoping against hope that he'd seen it wrong. His final marks have come in, and they're mediocre at best. It's the lowest grade he's ever gotten in an English class, all the way back to spelling test days in first grade. And the Philosophy grade. He can't look at it, knows he should feel the full weight of failure, but somehow can only think of how he just barely passed. Good enough.

Pushing away from his desk, he finds distance doesn't help the view. Good enough. That's who he is now—the guy who's just good enough.

His mother breezes into the room, and something inside tells him to frantically exit out of the page, to hide and lie, but he can't make himself move. It's too much effort. He listens instead to the sound of her laying out clean clothes on his blue plaid comforter, humming to herself.

"What're you up to today?"

He shrugs.

"Why didn't you go down to the lake?"

He shrugs.

"Hmph." She straightens, arms finally free of

cotton shirts and jeans. He knows she's stealing glances at his computer; she's never been overly sneaky about it. Her hand rests on his shoulder. "What's this?"

"Grades," he says, standing.

She maneuvers in front of him to get a better look, and he slips from the room, as if he can somehow escape the coming storm if he puts distance between them now. Like a fisherman outrunning a hurricane.

"Carson!"

As he dives into the kitchen, Amy and Anneliese arch their eyebrows in surprise from the dining room table. Feigning innocence, Carson opens the fridge, inspecting its contents as his mother marches in behind him.

"Do you mind explaining to me what I just saw?"

"It was a tough semester," he mutters.

"*Tough*? You're a good student, Carson. I just don't understand it."

He frowns at the mustard. "What's to understand? I nearly failed. There."

"Don't just stand there and shrug your shoulders at me! This's serious! You've never gotten grades like this. What've you been doing over there?" She sucks in a breath, and he braces himself. "I *knew* it was too much. You're too far from home."

His throat constricts, and he straightens, closing the fridge with a slam. Seeing his grades today made the prospect of returning to Oxford seem all but dreadful. How could he face going back? But that's *his* decision, and his mother standing there with her hands imperiously on her hips only infuriates him.

"How many times do I have to say it?" he roars. "I'm not going to school here!"

"Well, I'm not paying through the nose so that you can get grades like this! Do you think I like spending this much money so you can be so far away?"

He flees, from his mother, from the girls, staring at him through their lashes—flees out the backdoor and sees Jake and Mark down at the lake. They see him first, turning away stiffly. Scowling, Carson marches farther down the path to their neighbor's dock.

The old, mossy boards creak under his weight, and his body shivers, his breath coming out in wispy clouds. Shoving his hands into his pockets, Carson hunches his shoulders and, in spite of himself, pouts.

He's half-frozen by the time he hears someone coming up behind him. One of his coats gets draped over a shoulder as his father comes to stand beside him, an open beer bottle in his other hand.

He waits a long moment before caving and shoving his arms through the coat sleeves.

"She's impossible," he mumbles.

His father bobs his head in a small nod. "Your mother's proud of you, Carson."

"She's got a funny way of showing it."

"She just worries."

"Well, she shouldn't."

"No?" His father looks about. "You mean you haven't had the personality of a cactus this whole time?"

Carson winces from the sting of it and looks away. "I don't mean to ruin Christmas."

"Don't be dramatic," his father says. "If you really wanted to ruin it, you wouldn't have come home."

"Probably would've been better if I hadn't."

"Why?"

He doesn't answer, because he hasn't one.

"Will you tell me what's really bothering you? I know it can't be easy getting those grades, not when you've been so good in school, but it happened for a reason."

He shakes his head.

His father takes a sip from the bottle. "Your mother's got a point, though. I don't want you to have to worry about paying anything—I want the best for you. But if this isn't the best fit, then . . . "

"You think I should come back to school here."

"Do you want to?"

"No. I mean . . . I don't know."

His father's hand is heavy and warm when it rests on his shoulder. "Be honest with me. Is it too much? There's nothing wrong with feeling that way—it's a big change."

Carson sighs. "In some ways, I guess. I just . . . "

His father drapes an arm over his shoulders and pulls him into a sideways hug. "I think you should go back."

"Yeah?" he says in surprise.

"Mm."

"But what about—?"

"Don't worry about anything, alright? Just focus on school and getting used to things. You'll figure it out—I know you will. Just give it a little time."

Carson's chest expands in a long breath, his

father's words making him feel weightless and heavy all at once. "But what if I can't?"

His father takes a moment before answering, his weight shifting from one foot to the other. "All you can do is try."

Carson leans back in his chair, his stomach painfully full. Despite suffering through another of his mother's holiday hams, the side dishes were everything he missed about home. Remnants of garlic mashed potatoes, spiced carrots, green bean casserole, applesauce, and stuffed mushrooms litter everyone's plate, and his mother looks about with satisfied eyes at her overfull victims.

He barely contains a groan when Ellie rushes from the dinner table to fetch the worn Monopoly set as everyone begins clearing space on the checkered tablecloth for the board. Not sure if he can keep his eyes open five more minutes, let alone a whole Fields family round of Monopoly, Carson gratefully agrees when Anneliese asks if he'll walk with her.

Heavily coated and gloved, they head out the back door with his mother yelling to stick to the paths. The evening is streaked in lilac and violet, the North Star already full and bright. The moon is just beginning to crest over the Sierras, the top of its round face reflected in the dark, still waters of Lake Tahoe.

"Did you get enough to eat?"

Anneliese grins, amused. "Who didn't?"

He lets her take the lead, and her memory seems to have stayed true, since she easily finds her way down the path, onto a little square of beach fenced by two porous, gray boulders and a handful of tall trees. The sand crunches under their feet, one of the few noises out here in the cold Christmas night.

"You've been avoiding me," she says.

Wincing, he's happy she can't see his face very well. "I'm sorry."

"It's okay. I've been avoiding you, too, I think."

"Really?"

Her eyes, again amused, flick up to him. "Well, I haven't let Amy drag me all up and down the Sierra Nevadas for no reason."

"Ah. I'm sorry—you're on break, you shouldn't have to worry about avoiding me."

"You're on break too." Her face sinks into her scarf a little. "I really do appreciate you letting me come and paying for half the ticket. Nobody's ever done something like that for me."

"It's nothing."

She frowns at him. "It's not nothing. *You* shouldn't have to avoid *me*. This is your home, your family. This is your time away from everything. I didn't mean to ruin it."

"You didn't."

Fiddling with the end of her long braid, she says, "Then we should stop avoiding each other."

"That'd be best."

"Good."

A long moment passes before Carson plucks up the courage to say, "I'm sorry about that night. I didn't mean—"

She shakes her head. "It's my fault too. It was stupid. But you were there and being so nice and I just . . . wanted to be with you. But it didn't feel like I thought it would."

He can't quite muster anything to say, so he studies her from the corner of his eye, silently grateful for her putting into words what he's been struggling to. It didn't feel like he thought it would either. He's been wondering about Anneliese for so long, replaying their kiss in his head for so long, that in a way he thought that if he ever got the chance to do it again, do it right, everything would fit into place. He swallows hard at the next thought. It didn't feel like he thought it would, because it didn't feel right.

"Carson?" She says his name in a whisper. "Do you love me?"

"I want to."

She smiles sadly across the lake. "That's not really the same thing, is it?"

He shoves his hands in his pockets for something to do, unable to look at her. "I think I did, though," he says.

"I think I did too, back then. But . . . I'm not her anymore. And you're not the same anymore either."

He nods at the sand under his shoes.

"I think you should stop waiting for me."

A sort of numb calm washes over Carson then, and while he wants to be mad at her, to argue with her, his heart isn't in it. Because finally, someone voices what *is* right.

A lot of this past semester hasn't felt right, and he feels almost dizzy thinking of everything that's happened to him in only four months. But some things, *someone*, had seemed right. He frowns at the darkening lake, his thoughts crossing the Atlantic to an imagined nineteenth-century house in Bath.

He resurfaces from his thoughts when he hears Anneliese's voice.

"Do you think you could drive me somewhere on Monday?"

Putting the car into park and cranking the emergency break, Carson kills the engine. The sprawling concrete of the train station is fairly empty, only a few people with newspapers gracing the iron benches spread around.

Anneliese sits quietly in the passenger seat, biting a thumbnail, her eyes intent on the train tracks.

"Thanks for doing this."

He takes a relieved breath to hear that her voice, while not upbeat, isn't downcast either. His gaze swings over to her and he gives her his best encouraging grin.

"No problem. You're sure you want to go?"

She takes a moment, but nods. "I think I need to see him."

"My parents will come get you if you change your mind."

She smiles at him, though it doesn't quite reach her eyes.

"And you have all their numbers? And mine? And all the ones for Oxford?"

Nodding along, she says, "Yes, Carson, I have everything. I shouldn't be too far behind you getting back, but I'll probably miss the first few days. I'll let you know when I have a flight time."

He eases back into the seat, trying to be calm like she is. "You'll call me when you're there?"

"Yes."

"Anytime—don't worry about the time difference."

"No chance of that."

"Let me know if there's anything you need me to do at the college for you. I'll talk to professors or the dean or—"

"I know." She smiles again. "You're a good friend, Carson. Thank you."

"Sure thing."

Taking her hand in his, he lets a silence stretch between them because, for once, it's a comfortable silence. It reassures him. Though it pains him to be returning to Oxford without her, he understands that she wants to be with her father for a while.

"I'm also going to pay you back for that plane ticket."

"Don't worry about it."

"Carson . . . "

"Everything's taken care of," he says, squeezing her hand. "Just take your time—there's no rush."

She squeezes his hand back. "You, too, okay? No rush. Just take your time." She cracks a smile, but he can't quite manage one, so he leans across the center console and wraps his arms around her so she can't see his face. Leaning into him, she fills her fists with his jacket.

"I'm happy we found each other again," she says.

The loud clatter of the train pulling in tells them it's time. When she pulls back, her smile draws a matching one from him, and he's finally ready to let her go. With a nod she opens the passenger door, then pulls her suitcase from the backseat. Before she closes the passenger door, she leans back in and says, "I'll see you soon, okay?"

"You bet."

The firm slam of the passenger door has a finality to it. She waves to him from the train door. He waves back and watches as she heads in, her shoulders set.

And he sits there a moment longer after she and the train disappear, a golden oldie playing softly in the background from the radio.

The walk from Gloucester Green to Jesus College is somewhat surreal the second time around. No throng of anxious exchange students, no Ms. Billings reassuring parents. He walks with sure steps, taking the most direct route back to the college. Cornmarket is crowded with families and lingering Christmas tourists, and it takes him a while to push through with his laden shoulders.

As he walks down Ship Street to the front of the college, he smiles to remember his departure from SFO, just over twelve hours before. This time the whole Fields brood came, and they'd had to take the unsightly minivan to accommodate them all. Goodbyes took so long that other travelers had begun to stare, especially when Ellie began loudly telling him her next English gift wish list.

The hardest goodbye had, surprisingly, been his mother's. After his father released him from a bearish hug, his mother was at his elbow, a sort of resignation in her demeanor. He pulled her to him, and she hooked her chin over his shoulder.

"Go get 'em, baby."

"Will do," he said, smiling. He rested his chin on the top of her head and hugged tighter.

He also thinks of the hour he waited at the airport gate texting with Anneliese. She had settled alright in her father's apartment and thought she'd only be a week late to classes.

He enters through Jesus's main gate, smiling at the neatly dressed woman behind the custodian's desk. As he and his duffel make their way through the quadrangles, deeper into the college, Carson realizes everything is familiar—every turn, every stone. It's kind of like coming home, too.

He smiles to see Anders, his blonde head poking out of his room at the sound of the front door opening.

Taking the hand Anders extends, Carson nods at the inquiry about his holidays.

"Pretty good. Yours?"

"No complaints, though the weather was bloody abysmal."

"Well it *is* England," he says, grinning innocently at Anders's mockingly dark look for that remark.

"Some of us are going out tonight," Anders says as Carson fits the keycard into his door's lock. "You game?"

"Next time," Carson promises.

Anders agrees with an easy nod and slips back into his room, leaving the door propped open.

Carson enters his own room, finding it just as he left it, if a little neater. After letting his duffel drop unceremoniously onto the bed, he goes about heating water, pillaging the restocked tea tray. While the tea steeps, he munches on a cookie and unpacks.

He places the clothes in the wardrobe, hanging up the new soccer jersey Jake and Amy bought him for Christmas with a smile.

"It'll help you *assimilate,*" Jake said with a grin, showing off his latest vocabulary word.

He pins up Ellie's present, a hand drawing of what she imagines Jesus College looks like, on the corkboard behind his desk. With that done and his tea ready, Carson sits down at his desk.

He'd jotted down some plotlines for a new story on the plane over, and his fingers itch to flesh out some rudimentary character sketches. The cursor blinks at him, but as the words come flowing across the page, he finds they aren't a new story at all but an apology. He's done this a few times before, committing to paper what his voice can't speak up and say. He explains to Mandy what he did, why he thinks he did it, and that he never meant to hurt her. He knows she'll never see this letter—he intends to click NO when Word asks if he wants to save changes to the document—but it helps him form a short text to her:

I know this is late, but I hope you know that I'm sorry. I didn't mean for everything to get messed up. I'd like to explain everything, but I understand if you'd rather not. It was my fault and I'm sorry.

It takes a while for his fingers to work their way across the keyboard, but he pushes through. Though a lump forms in his throat when he presses SEND, a weight lifts off his shoulders.

He bustles around the room to distract himself, knowing he shouldn't expect a text back at all, let alone quickly.

So the alert from his phone almost startles him.

He leans over the desk and smiles.

Hey.